THE PRESIDENT'S CHOICE

SAFETY AND SECURITY

DENIS JAMES

Dedications & Acknowledgements

I've always loved a good "what if" story. What if things played out just a little bit differently? How could one choice spiral into a cascade of differences between two seemingly similar structures?

This is far from "the same story twice". No, these are two completely different paths taken based on our values and choices. Our values and choices determine our journey in life.

Thank you to those who inspired me to answer the question, "what if we had chosen to do things differently?" Thank you to those who surprised me even when I thought I knew them. (That is both good and bad, by the way!) Thank you to those who remain consistent no matter the circumstances, that's tough to do sometimes. Thank you to those who are always authentically themselves. And thank you, to me, for no longer being afraid to be who I am.

To anyone who's ever had to choose between the safe lie and the dangerous truth. Your courage matters, even when no one else sees it.

Thank you all.

Much love,

Denis James

Contents

Chapter One

The January air was crisp and biting as Jordan Prescott stood on the steps of the Capitol Building, her right hand raised. Frost glittered on the marble columns behind her, and her breath formed small clouds with each exhale. In the distance, she could see the Washington Monument piercing a sky so blue it seemed artificial. Thousands of people filled the National Mall, a sea of faces turned expectantly toward her—many bearing signs with messages like "Madam President At Last" and "History Made Today."

The Chief Justice, Eleanor Hayes (no relation to Asher, Jordan had checked), stood opposite her, her weathered face solemn as she held the Bible. Her voice, amplified by microphones, carried across the hushed crowd.

"Please repeat after me," the Chief Justice said, her tone formal but warm. "I, Jordan Elaine Prescott..."

Jordan drew a deep breath, acutely aware of the weight of history pressing down on her shoulders. This was the same oath taken by Washington, Lincoln, Roosevelt—and now her, the first woman to stand in this spot for this purpose. The responsibility was staggering.

"I, Jordan Elaine Prescott, do solemnly swear that I will faithfully execute the Office of President of the United States, and will to the best of my ability, preserve, protect and defend the Constitution of the United States, so help me God."

The Chief Justice nodded solemnly. "Congratulations, Madam President."

A twenty-one-gun salute thundered across the mall, making some jump in the crowd. The military struck up "Hail to the Chief," and the crowd erupted in applause—some enthusiastic, others more restrained. Jordan maintained her composure, offering a reserved smile rather than the exuberant wave many politicians might have given. As the standard-bearer for the Progressive Alliance party, she had campaigned on a platform of measured reform and ethical governance. The people hadn't elected her for theatrics; they'd chosen her for her unflinching dedication to justice and order.

Jordan approached the podium for her inaugural address, adjusting the microphone slightly. She looked out at the crowd—not at the teleprompter—as she began.

"My fellow Americans, I stand before you today not as the victor of a partisan contest, but as a servant entrusted with a sacred duty." Her voice was clear and steady, carrying the same authoritative tone that had made her such an effective prosecutor. "Our nation faces challenges that transcend party lines—economic uncertainty, threats both foreign and domestic, and a sense of division that has too often defined our discourse."

She paused, allowing her gaze to sweep across the crowd. Supporters of the Progressive Alliance cheered, while members of the Conservative Covenant stood with arms folded, skeptical but listening.

"I make this vow to every citizen, regardless of whether you cast your ballot for me: I will govern with integrity. I will pursue justice without favor. And I will never forget that I serve all Americans."

As Jordan continued her speech, she noticed several things simultaneously. Her security detail seemed unusually spread out, with gaps in coverage at the edges of the platform. A flash of movement caught her eye—a man in a maintenance uniform was being waved through a checkpoint with only a cursory ID check. And at the far edge of the VIP section, a figure in a dark coat was watching her with unusual intensity.

Brushing off her security concerns for the moment, Jordan concluded her speech with a call for unity and purpose that earned a standing ovation from most in attendance. As she stepped away from the podium, she turned to shake hands with Theo Marshall, her Vice President.

Theo was younger than her by nearly a decade, with an easy charm that balanced her more austere demeanor. His dark skin contrasted with the bright white of his smile as he leaned in to speak privately with her.

"We did it, Madam President," he said, grinning broadly, his voice carrying a hint of his Louisiana upbringing. "Not bad for a prosecutor and a professor, huh? And they said America would never elect a woman."

"The hard part starts now," she replied, though she allowed herself a brief, genuine smile. "I'll need your help, Theo. More than I ever did on the campaign."

"You've got it," he said, his expression becoming serious for a moment. "Whatever comes our way."

As they moved through the formal proceedings, Jordan surveyed the dignitaries assembled on the platform. Finn Sullivan, her newly appointed Press Secretary, stood nearby, already fielding questions from reporters with the casual confidence that had made him a rising star in political communications. At thirty-five, Finn was considered young for the position, but his uncanny ability to deflect hostile questions while maintaining an air of complete transparency had impressed Jordan during the campaign.

He caught her eye and gave a subtle nod—everything was proceeding as planned. But Jordan noticed a tightness around his eyes that hadn't been there earlier. Something was bothering him.

The presidential parade would begin soon, followed by the inaugural balls. Jordan had insisted on limiting these to three—far fewer than previous administrations—citing the expense and her desire to get to work immediately. This practical approach had resonated with voters tired of political pageantry.

Evelyn Harper, Jordan's former rival from the Conservative Covenant party, approached with a gracious smile that didn't quite reach her eyes. Their campaign had been contentious but largely respectful. Evelyn had conceded with dignity once the results were clear, though her concession speech had contained a barely veiled warning about "vigilance against overreach."

At fifty-seven, Evelyn was slightly older than Jordan, with a political career spanning three decades. Where Jordan was known for her direct, no-nonsense approach, Evelyn cultivated a warm, maternal image that belied her shrewd political instincts.

"Congratulations, Madam President," Evelyn said, extending her hand. "I trust you'll remember that forty-eight percent of the country voted for a different vision."

"I represent all Americans now, Senator Harper," Jordan replied evenly. "My door will always be open for constructive dialogue."

"I hope so," Evelyn said, lowering her voice. "Because there are forces at work that won't be satisfied with dialogue alone. And they certainly won't be pleased with the... precedent... your election has set. Be careful, Jordan." Before Jordan could ask what she meant, Evelyn had moved away to greet other dignitaries.

Jordan found herself momentarily unsettled by the cryptic warning. Was it merely the bitter aftertaste of a hard-fought campaign, or something more specific?

As Evelyn moved away, an aide approached with a small velvet box. "Madam President, the First Ladies Historical Association asked me to present this to you. They said it was meant for this day."

Jordan opened the box to find an antique silver brooch, crafted in the shape of a key. A small card explained: "For the woman who unlocked the highest door. With respect and admiration."

She pinned it discreetly to her lapel, touched by the gesture but uncomfortable with too much focus on the historical nature of her election. She had always wanted to be judged on her merits, not her gender.

Jordan frowned slightly as she observed a security detail allowing a group of donors past a checkpoint with minimal screening. One man caught her attention—he wore the correct clearance badge, but it seemed slightly off-center, as if recently attached. The guard barely glanced at it before waving him through.

She made a mental note to discuss security protocols with the Secret Service director. The White House security appeared laxer than she would prefer, particularly given the current polarized political climate and Silas's vague warning.

The parade was beginning to form on Pennsylvania Avenue. Jordan would need to make her way to the presidential limousine soon. As she prepared to leave the platform, she caught sight of a woman in the crowd, staring directly at her with an intensity that seemed out of place amid the celebration. For a moment, their eyes locked, and Jordan felt an inexplicable chill. The woman's face was partially obscured by a scarf, but her eyes seemed familiar somehow.

Then the woman was gone, swallowed by the crowd as Jordan was ushered toward the waiting vehicle.

The remainder of the ceremony passed in a blur of handshakes, photographs, and carefully scripted remarks. Jordan attended the first inaugural ball long enough to share the traditional first dance with her husband, Michael, a professor of constitutional law who preferred to remain in the background of her political life. After a brief appearance at the other two balls, she begged off further celebrations.

"The country doesn't need me to dance," she told her staff. "It needs me to work."

By late afternoon, Jordan found herself in the Oval Office—her office now—taking in the weight of her new responsibility. The room was quieter than she had expected, almost reverent in its stillness. She ran her fingers along the edge of the Resolute Desk, thinking of all the decisions that had been made there, for better or worse.

A small, framed note caught her eye, something that hadn't been there during her transition team visits. She picked it up and read the handwritten message from former President Reed: "Jordan—The burden is heavier for the ones who break the ceiling. Remember why you're here. —J.R."

She had just settled behind the desk when the phone rang. The caller ID showed it was Liam Bennett, her Executive Assistant. Liam had been with Jordan from the beginning—first as a close friend in college, then as campaign manager, and now as her right hand in the White House. He was one of Jordan's closest friends, yet they disagreed on nearly every policy. They'd spent countless nights debating political issues over drinks. While Jordan didn't select Liam as VP, having someone close who respectfully challenged viewpoints seemed essential. In her opinion, it was good to keep another perspective close at hand.

"Executive Assistant Bennett," Jordan answered, barely containing the smile in her voice. "Wow, that feels good--"

"Not to rain on your parade, but we have a situation." Liam's voice sounded uncharacteristically tense. "You need to make your way to the conference room. Immediately. Please."

Jordan's smile faded. It was quite unlike Liam to be this serious, especially today. The inauguration just happened hours ago. Surely an emergency couldn't occur so quickly into her term.

"What are you talking about, Liam?"

"I'm not going to explain over the phone. Just come down to the conference room."

The dial tone indicated Liam had hung up. Concerned, Jordan placed the receiver down and headed for the door. As she made her way to the conference room, her mind cycled through possibilities. A contested election result? Unlikely, Evelyn had already conceded. Something from the past as a prosecuting attorney? She'd maintained a 95% conviction rate but had always played by the rules. Nothing from her school days would rise to this level of concern.

Within minutes, Jordan arrived at the conference room. Taking a deep breath, she pushed open the door. Inside, she found four people sitting around the long table. All four turned to face her as she entered.

"Ah, good, you're here," Liam said, rising from his chair. He walked over and closed the door behind her. As he did so, he whispered, "I'm so sorry this is happening on your first day."

Jordan took in the room, recognizing the faces immediately. The first was Jasper Reed, her predecessor who had declined to seek re-election. She'd had minimal contact with Jasper, though she knew the public respected him greatly and likely would have re-elected him had he run.

The second was Aria Collins, her National Security Advisor. Jordan had appointed Aria herself, based on her outstanding reputation in intelligence circles. With twenty years in various security agencies, Aria was known for her unflinching assessments and no-nonsense approach. Her silver-streaked black hair was pulled back in a tight bun, and her dark eyes missed nothing. She wore the same expression Jordan had seen during briefings: alert, calculating, and slightly grim.

The third person, surprisingly, was a teenager: Nina Foster. Now fourteen, Nina was less than a year old when she was abducted by the infamous terrorist organization known as "The Purists," led by a man named Asher Hayes. The entire country had been told, years before Jasper took office, that Hayes was dead. Shot and killed on live television, in fact.

To say The Purists were a terrorist organization was putting it mildly. During Asher's reign, terror and chaos dominated national life. The mere mention of "The Purists" could empty streets and cause panic attacks among those who lived through those dark years. Hayes preached that only heterosexual white males deserved freedom, calling them "the pure ones," and after years of spreading this ideology through underground networks and encrypted online platforms, he eventually convinced his followers to begin what he termed the "Great Purification"—violent eradication of those he deemed "impure."

Thousands of armed Purists took to the streets wearing their distinctive white masks emblazoned with a single red teardrop, assaulting homosexuals, women, and people of color. For over a year, police were overwhelmed by widespread violence. People were terrified to leave their homes. Many of Hayes's followers had infiltrated law enforcement and military positions, often arresting victims instead of perpetrators. The Purists were known for their signature method of terrorism: they would target a neighborhood, cut all communication, and systematically hunt down residents who didn't fit their twisted ideology.

Jordan remembered those days vividly. As a young assistant district attorney, she had prosecuted several members of The Purists who had been caught during raids. She still occasionally had nightmares about the evidence she'd had to review—the photos, the videos, the testimony from survivors. One case haunted her to this day: a Purist who had infiltrated a hospital posing as an emergency room provider. Somehow, he managed to "convince" the other personnel that he was the new attending physician, and subsequently denied treatment to anyone who was not a white male. Conveniently, there had been a massive pile-up on the freeway that day (suspected cause: another Purist) that resulted in hundreds of people being life flighted to the same hospital. The only survivors were the "pure" ones. The man had shown no remorse, only quoting Hayes's manifesto during his testimony. "The pure shall inherit the earth," he had said, smiling at Jordan across the courtroom.

Nina's kidnapping changed everything. When word spread that Hayes himself had abducted an infant, public outrage galvanized resistance. What looked like the second Civil War erupted in the streets as people emerged from hiding and overwhelmed The Purists, resulting in their deaths, arrests, or retreat into hiding.

Nina was found in a church the next day and taken to an orphanage; her parents having been killed by Hayes. News outlets broadcast footage of Asher Hayes being shot and killed by police, and the violence virtually ended after that. The country began a slow healing process, though the trauma of The Purists' reign remained an open wound in the national psyche.

"Liam," Jordan began, but Jasper raised a hand.

"Nina wishes to speak to you directly, President Prescott," he said quietly.

Jordan turned to Nina, who took a deep breath before words poured out. "I saw him, President Prescott. Asher Hayes. He's very much alive."

The room fell silent as Jordan processed this statement. She studied Nina carefully, noting the girl's trembling hands and the dark circles under her eyes. Jordan had built her career on being able to read witnesses, to separate truth from fiction in high-pressure situations. Nina genuinely believed what she was saying—but how could it be true?

"What do you mean, Nina?" she asked gently.

"I mean, he's alive. I saw him! He tried to kidnap me again!" Nina's voice cracked slightly.

"Tell me exactly what happened."

"I was walking home from school—well, to the orphanage—when a car pulled up beside me. A man rolled down the window and asked if I wanted a ride." Tears welled in Nina's eyes. "I turned to decline—stranger danger and all that. But it was him, President. I've studied his face in the news for years, trying to understand why he did what he did. That was Asher Hayes, without a doubt."

"Did he say anything else to you?" Jordan asked, her prosecutor's instincts kicking in.

Nina hesitated, then nodded slowly. "He said... he said, 'You've grown up nicely, little one.' That's what he used to call me when he had me. Little one. No one knows that." She hugged herself, as if trying to hold the memory at bay. "Then he said, 'Tell Jordan I said hello.' He knew you were President. This happened yesterday, before your inauguration was official."

Jordan felt a chill run through her. If Hayes was alive and knew she was becoming President before it was official, that suggested either an intelligence network or something more disturbing.

She turned to Jasper. "What do you make of this?"

Jasper frowned. "I'm not sure," he admitted. "Asher Hayes predates my administration. I never thought of requesting briefings on him, and now I lack authority. That's in your hands now."

Liam interjected, "I've already requested all records relating to Asher Hayes from Aria. But here's the strange part: all files on Asher Hayes have been destroyed."

"What do you mean?" Jordan asked, her concern deepening.

"There are no records on him. We have no official information."

"How is that possible? The government must have kept detailed files during that chaos. I was just starting as an attorney then—it was absolute pandemonium!"

"I agree," Liam said quickly. "But the records are gone. Someone ordered them destroyed."

"It wasn't me," Jasper added promptly.

Jordan turned to Aria, who had remained silent until now. "Aria, what can you tell me about this?"

Aria Collins straightened in her chair; her posture military precise. "Madam President, I've been reviewing what little we have left. Most official records were indeed purged from our systems approximately nine years ago. However, I've been able to piece together some information from archived news reports and personal accounts."

She opened a thin folder on the table. "Asher Hayes founded The Purists in 1994, initially as a fringe hate group. By 1998, they had grown into a full-blown domestic terrorist organization with cells in every major city. Their violence peaked in 1999-2000, which is when Nina was abducted. Hayes was reportedly killed in February 2000."

Aria's expression grew more serious. "What concerns me, however, are the inconsistencies in the official death report. The body was cremated within hours—highly unusual protocol. The officer who signed off on Hayes's death certificate disappeared two weeks later. And three key witnesses to his shooting later recanted their testimonies, claiming memory lapses."

"So, is it possible? Could he still be alive?" Jordan asked.

The footage of Asher Hayes's death had been broadcast continuously for weeks in 2000. Jordan remembered watching it in her small apartment the night it aired. The helicopter camera followed Hayes as police cornered him outside an abandoned church in Maryland. He'd been surrounded, red laser sights dancing across his white shirt.

When the order to surrender was ignored, twenty-three officers opened fire simultaneously. The video captured it all—Hayes staggering backward, his body jerking with impacts before collapsing onto blood-soaked pavement. The shooter who approached for confirmation placed two fingers to Hayes's neck, then shook his head at the camera. CNN had replayed that shake of the head hundreds of times: the moment America's most wanted terrorist was confirmed dead.

What haunted Jordan in that moment was remembering her own reaction. She'd celebrated that night. Popped a bottle of cheap champagne with fellow prosecutors. They'd tracked Purist cases for months. This was justice served.

Now, reading through Aria's files, Jordan discovered why memories of that footage felt wrong. They'd been edited. Frame-by-frame analysis showed digital manipulation—seamless, but detectable with current technology. The blood didn't splatter correctly. The body jerked at impossible angles. The approaching officer's head shake was too smooth, too perfect.

Most disturbing: no coroner's report existed. Hayes's body had been "cremated for national security reasons" within hours. No autopsy. No tissue samples. No DNA confirmation.

"The archived footage was manipulated," Aria explained, pointing to micro-inconsistencies. "Someone with incredible resources wanted us to see Hayes die. But these artifacts suggest the original video might have captured something... different."

"Different how?"

"We can't know. The original footage was apparently destroyed in a server fire three days after broadcast. Only this version remains."

"And what of the...rumors?"

There were rumors about Asher Hayes. That he was somehow... not entirely human. More than one conspiracy theorist prophesized that the man was capable of far more than any human. Hayes's reign of terror was riddled with unexplained phenomena—disappearances that defied logic, security footage that would mysteriously corrupt, and witnesses who would suddenly develop gaps in their memory.

Jordan had always dismissed these stories as exaggerations born from the trauma of that period. But there was one incident during a trial... A key witness against a high-ranking Purist had been in protective custody, guarded by officers Jordan had personally vetted. The building had state-of-the-art security, with no blind spots in its camera coverage. Yet somehow, the witness had vanished from a locked room. The security footage showed nothing but static for precisely three minutes and fourteen seconds. When the image returned, the room was empty. No doors or windows had been opened. The witness was never found, the case had collapsed, and Jordan had never been able to explain what happened.

Aria's expression remained carefully neutral, but Jordan noticed her knuckles whitening as she gripped her pen. "Madam President, I deal in facts, not rumors. But I will say this: during The Purists' reign, there were tactical decisions made by Hayes that defied conventional explanation. He seemed to anticipate security measures before they were implemented. He appeared in locations where he couldn't possibly have known to be. And..." she hesitated.

"Go on," Jordan urged.

"And there were sixteen documented cases of individuals who claimed to have personally killed Hayes, only to find him still operational elsewhere. Sixteen separate, credible reports of his death before the final, 'official' one."

Nina nodded vigorously. "That's because he's not normal. He can do things. Things no one should be able to do."

"What should we do?" Liam asked. He sounded panicky. "If we do nothing, we're potentially putting the country at risk. Asher Hayes is an incredibly dangerous man." Jordan recalled Liam had lost his parents to the Purists as well. This was likely hitting close to home for him. She sympathized with her friend, though couldn't help feeling a little frustrated with his panic in this moment.

"Hold on," Aria interrupted. "The word of a fourteen-year-old girl obsessed with her parents' murder suddenly claiming to see a dead man may not convince everyone. When Hayes was active, things were... catastrophic. People were terrified. We cannot announce 'That terrorist we told you was dead is actually alive' without absolute proof."

"What kind of proof do you need?" Liam snapped. "Dead bodies? What's the harm in warning the public?"

"The harm," Aria explained deliberately, "is mass panic. You may not remember those times, but the terror was paralyzing. If we announce Hayes is back without concrete evidence, we'll have riots within hours. People will barricade themselves in their homes. There will be vigilante groups forming by nightfall. The economic impact alone—markets crashing, businesses closing—would be devastating."

Jasper nodded in agreement. "The mere mention of The Purists still triggers PTSD in millions of citizens. Last year, a college student's thesis on that period caused three hospitalizations just from the reading material."

Nina looked furious but remained silent, arms crossed as she glared at Aria.

"You don't believe me," she finally said. "None of you actually believe me."

"It's not about believing you, Nina," Jordan said carefully. "It's about ensuring we have enough evidence before taking actions that would affect the entire country."

Nina reached into her pocket and pulled out a small object, placing it on the table. It was a white button with a single red teardrop painted on it.

"He dropped this when I ran. It fell from his jacket. That's a Purist button—they all wore these under their collars. It was like their secret identifier."

Aria picked up the button carefully with a pen, examining it. "This looks authentic, but it could be a replica. There are collectors of... dark memorabilia."

"Check for fingerprints," Nina insisted. "He touched it. I know he did."

Liam leaned forward. "Even if we investigate quietly and find nothing, what's the harm? But if we say nothing and Hayes is back? He could be rebuilding his network as we speak. The Purists went underground, but they never truly disbanded. There are still sympathizers out there. If we conduct a quiet investigation and he realizes we're onto him, he could accelerate whatever plans he has."

"Or worse," Aria added, her voice dropping, "if he truly possesses the... abilities... that people claimed, he might already know we're having this conversation."

The room fell silent at that chilling thought.

"There's something else," Nina said quietly. "Something I didn't tell you before because I was scared you'd think I was making it up." She pulled out her phone, hands shaking slightly. "I took this yesterday. After he drove away."

She pulled up a photo and placed the phone on the table. The image was blurry, taken hastily, but it showed a black car driving away. The license plate was partially visible, and through the rear window, the back of a man's head could be seen—white hair with a distinctive streak of black running from the crown to the nape.

"Hayes had that exact hair pattern," Aria said, her professional demeanor cracking slightly. "It was quite distinctive. We used it to identify him in surveillance footage."

"Madam President," Aria continued after a moment, "I need to be clear about the risks. If we announce Hayes's potential return without solid evidence, we face nationwide panic, economic disruption, and potential riots. If we keep this quiet and investigate, we risk giving him time to operate unimpeded. And the third option—doing nothing—risks allowing a dangerous terrorist to potentially rebuild his network if Nina's account is accurate."

"There's also the political fallout to consider," Jasper added. "If you announce Hayes is back and it turns out to be false, your administration would never recover from the blow to its credibility. Your presidency would effectively be over before it began."

"And if I say nothing and he kills more people?" Jordan asked pointedly.

No one had an answer to that.

Jordan rose from her chair and walked to the window, looking out at the city below. Citizens going about their daily lives, completely unaware of the potential threat that might be re-emerging. She'd sworn to protect these people just hours ago. Now she faced an impossible choice: risk nationwide panic and possibly her entire presidency on the testimony of a teenager and a blurry photo, or conduct a quiet investigation that might give a dangerous terrorist time to rebuild his network of hate.

She thought of the chaos during The Purists' reign. As a young prosecutor, she'd seen the aftermath of their attacks—broken families, traumatized survivors, communities torn apart by fear and suspicion. The thought of that happening again made her stomach turn.

But she also remembered something her mentor had told her early in her career: "The easiest way to make a bad situation worse is to act without sufficient information." It was against her nature to announce a threat she couldn't prove existed—her entire career had been built on evidence, facts, and methodical procedure.

Yet as she looked at Nina, she saw a girl who had already lost everything to this man. If Hayes truly was back and targeting Nina again, how could she not act immediately?

Jordan returned to the table, her decision crystallizing. "Aria, if we were to investigate quietly, how would we proceed?"

"I'd assemble a small, elite team—people I trust implicitly. We'd establish surveillance at key locations associated with former Purist activities. We'd monitor Nina's safety around the clock. And we'd discreetly reach out to former intelligence assets who specialized in tracking Hayes."

"How long would this take?"

"To get concrete evidence? A week at minimum. Maybe longer."

"And if we go public immediately?"

Jasper answered, "We'd need to implement emergency protocols nationwide. Curfews, increased police presence, possibly even National Guard deployment in major cities. The panic would be immediate and severe."

"There's something else to consider," Liam added quietly. "If Hayes is truly back and has the same... capabilities... as before, going public might force him underground, making him harder to catch. A quiet investigation might give us the element of surprise."

"Or," Nina interjected, her voice trembling slightly, "he could take more children while you're busy investigating. He told me yesterday that 'the purification would begin again soon.' He's planning something, and soon."

The weight of the decision pressed down on Jordan's shoulders. This wasn't how she had imagined her first day in office would go. She looked at Nina's determined face, then at Jasper's concerned expression, Aria's calculating gaze, and finally at Liam's expectant look.

She knew that whatever she decided would have far-reaching consequences. If she sounded the alarm immediately, the country would plunge into panic and chaos, possibly for nothing if Nina was mistaken or manipulated. Markets would crash, violence would erupt, and the fragile social fabric that had taken years to repair after The Purists' reign would tear again. Her own presidency might not survive the backlash if she was wrong.

But if she opted for a quiet investigation and Hayes was truly back, he would have precious time to operate unimpeded. More lives could be lost. And if the public ever found out she had known of a possible threat and said nothing? The betrayal would be unforgivable.

After careful consideration, Jordan made her decision. The stakes were too high to act on impulse alone. She would need to balance immediate safety with the risk of widespread chaos.

"Here's what we're going to do," President Prescott announced, her voice steady with newfound resolve.

Chapter Two

Jordan Prescott remained at the window, watching traffic move like blood cells through the city's arteries. She'd sworn to protect all of this—the ordinary lives, the mundane routines that Hayes had once shattered with violence. Making this decision felt like choosing between the devil and the deep blue sea.

"We investigate in secret," she said finally, turning back to the room. "Aria, you'll lead." Relief flickered across faces, except for Jasper's, which remained carved from skepticism. "The team must be absolutely minimal," Jordan continued. "No one outside this room can know the true nature of what we're investigating."

"I have three candidates in mind," Aria said crisply. "Former Task Force Ghost members. They never believed Hayes was truly dead."

"Task Force Ghost?" Liam asked.

"Classified unit during the Purist crisis. Their funding evaporated after Hayes's reported death, but some continued investigating on their own time." Aria's fingers moved swiftly across her tablet. "Agent Vasquez spent years tracking unexplained incidents with Purist signatures. Detective Martinez still has contacts in communities that were hit hardest. Dr. Elena Reeves developed the psychological profile on Hayes—she always believed something was off about his death."

"I want them activated by morning," Jordan said. "Cover stories for everyone."

"School safety review," Liam suggested. "We're updating protocols for educational facilities, youth centers, orphanages."

"Perfect. Gives us legitimate access to records, locations, personnel." Aria was already typing. "I'll draft the executive order establishing the review committee."

"And Nina?" Jasper asked pointedly. "If Hayes is watching her, constant protection will signal we're onto him."

Nina spoke before Jordan could respond. "I can handle school. I'll act normal. Just... keep someone nearby?"

"I'm assigning Agent Chen as your new guidance counselor at school," Aria told her. "Former CIA, speaks three languages. If Hayes approaches again, she'll know."

Jordan paced behind her chair. "The orphanage staff needs vetting. Hayes had operatives everywhere before."

"Already underway," Aria confirmed. "Background checks on everyone from the director to the weekend janitor. Medical records, financial history, travel patterns for the past five years."

"Communications monitoring?"

"Passive for now. If we find actual Purist chatter, we'll escalate." Aria looked up from her tablet. "There's something else. The license plate in Nina's photo—my team ran preliminary scans. It's not just any car." The room focused on her. "Government vehicle. State Department pool. Checked out yesterday to..." She paused. "Senator Evelyn Harper's office."

Silence stretched uncomfortably. "There could be explanations," Jasper offered stiffly.

"Of course." Aria's professional neutrality never wavered. "We'll need to investigate quietly. If Senator Harper is involved—"

"She's not," Jordan cut in firmly. Then, more carefully: "But we follow every lead."

"The destroyed files worry me more," Liam admitted. "Who had that kind of clearance?"

"Limited list," Jasper said. "President, AG, heads of intelligence agencies, maybe a handful of others."

"You included, Mr. President," Aria noted carefully.

Jasper's face reddened. "I never authorized destroying Hayes's files. But..." He frowned. "My final year in office is somewhat fragmented in my memory. Stress, age, the burden of transition planning. I approved hundreds of documents daily."

"We need to review all classified executive orders from that period," Jordan decided. "Cross-reference with personnel movements, security logs, anything that might indicate who really ordered the purge."

"That could take weeks," Aria warned.

"Start with the week of Harper's latest visit to the State Department," Jordan suggested. "See if there's any unusual activity around the records department."

A knock interrupted them. Finn Sullivan entered, looking apologetic. "Madam President? The media is asking about the extended meeting..."

"Tell them we're finalizing domestic security priorities," Jordan replied smoothly. "Planning our first hundred days."

"Of course." Finn hesitated. "Also, Senator Harper is requesting an urgent meeting. Something about national security matters that can't wait."

The room tensed.

"Tell her I'll call personally this evening," Jordan said. "After I've settled into the Oval Office."

When Finn left, Jordan addressed the group again. "This meeting ends now. Aria, begin immediate surveillance on former Purist locations. Liam, I need normal administration operations to continue seamlessly. Jasper, you're meeting with educational board members tomorrow about national standards—perfect cover to discuss security protocols."

"Evidence threshold?" Aria asked. "When do we go public?"

"Concrete, irrefutable proof. Multiple sources. Physical evidence. Video that can't be faked." Jordan's voice dropped. "Until then, Hayes is a ghost."

As they dispersed, Nina lingered. "What if he contacts me again?" Jordan gripped the girl's thin shoulder. The weight of responsibility pressed down—Nina was the key to unraveling this mystery or destroying her presidency entirely. "Record everything. Remember everything. We're counting on you."

Alone in the Oval Office afterward, Jordan sank into the presidential chair. Her first day had been consumed by potential phantoms and impossible choices. The afternoon sun cast long shadows across the room where so many critical decisions had been made. Her secure phone buzzed. Aria: "First surveillance team deployed. Watching the former safe house on Kingman Street. Nothing yet." Jordan typed back: "Continue pattern. Expand tomorrow." Another message arrived: "Forensics preliminary on Nina's photo. Image appears authentic, not digitally altered. Car registration matches Harper's office records." Jordan closed her eyes. Either Nina's trauma had created an elaborate delusion, or the country faced a threat more dangerous than anything since the original Purist crisis. And she was betting everything on one frightened teenager's testimony.

Her other phone rang. The caller ID showed Evelyn Harper's office. "Madam President," Harper's voice was warm but strained.

"Congratulations on your first day. I won't take much of your time, but there's something urgent we need to discuss. In person, if possible."

"Of course, Senator. Shall we say tomorrow morning?" "Actually..." Harper lowered her voice. "This can't wait. Could I come to the White House now? Back entrance, minimal security? It's about something you need to know before—"

"Before what?"

"Before you make any... irrevocable decisions. Decisions that might harm the country. Or yourself." A chill ran through Jordan. "One hour. Second floor study. Minimal staff." She ended the call and immediately messaged Aria: "Harper meeting tonight. Full surveillance. Record everything."

The next hour crawled by as Jordan reviewed briefing materials, trying to appear occupied with normal presidential duties while her mind raced with possibilities. When Harper arrived, escorted by a single aide, she looked older than at the inauguration. Dark circles shadowed her eyes.

"Please," Jordan indicated chairs by the fireplace. "What couldn't wait?" Harper glanced at her aide, who remained by the door. "I know about Nina Foster." Jordan's expression remained neutral. "I'm not sure what you—"

"Please." Harper leaned forward. "I know because I've been watching her. Not in any nefarious way, but because I recognized the signs." She paused, choosing words carefully. "I have a sister. Bella. Brilliant, beautiful. She developed an... obsession with a case my father prosecuted years ago. She started seeing connections everywhere. Convinced herself people involved weren't dead, that they were following her."

"Where is she now?"

"Psychiatric facility. Third year of her commitment." Harper's voice caught. "The delusions were so real to her. So vivid. She passed every polygraph because she truly believed."

Jordan processed this carefully. "Why are you telling me this?"

"Because," Harper said slowly, "before Bella's breakdown, she began researching Asher Hayes. She was convinced he survived. She found discrepancies in the death reports, collected evidence, interviewed survivors. The similarity to what I've heard about Nina is... striking."

"Heard from whom?"

Harper smiled sadly. "You think I don't have sources? My car was flagged leaving the orphanage vicinity yesterday. I went there checking on a child I sponsor. I heard about Nina's episode, the claims about Hayes. I may be your opposition, Jordan, but I won't let you destroy your presidency over a troubled girl's trauma."

"You're making assumptions."

"Am I? Then why are former Task Force Ghost members being quietly reactivated? Why are classified executive orders from my predecessor suddenly under review?" Harper stood, pacing to the window. "I spent eight years watching my sister destroy herself chasing ghosts. Don't let Nina Foster become your undoing."

"What are you suggesting?"

"Get her proper help. Psychiatric evaluation. Treatment. But don't..." Harper turned back. "Don't let her convince you to chase shadows." She pulled a folder from her briefcase. "These are Bella's files. The similarities to Nina's claims are... uncanny."

Jordan accepted the folder, noting Aria would analyze every page later. "Thank you for your concern, Evelyn. I assure you, any decisions I make will be in the country's best interests."

"I hope so." Harper paused at the door. "Because if Asher Hayes is truly alive, and you announce it without absolute proof, the panic will tear this country apart. And if he's dead, and you announce otherwise, your credibility dies with your presidency."

After Harper left, Jordan sat in darkness for long minutes, the folder unopened on her lap. Every instinct screamed that Nina was telling the truth, but doubt crept in like morning fog. Her phone buzzed. Aria: "Harper meeting recorded. Analyzing now." Another message followed: "Surveillance update: Movement detected at old Purist training ground. Team moving in." Jordan stood, decision crystallizing. Whether monster or madness, the investigation would continue. But now she had to consider another possibility—that multiple people across time might share the same delusion about Asher Hayes.

Chapter Three

The morning's presidential briefing covered standard foreign policy matters until Aria placed a sealed folder before Jordan. "Senator Harper's vehicle was logged near the orphanage at 4:47 PM—seventeen minutes before Nina's alleged Hayes encounter."

"Coincidence," Liam suggested, though his tone lacked conviction.

"Perhaps." Aria opened the file. "But this requires explanation. Harper entered a government property—Building 7 of the State Department archives—for thirty-seven minutes yesterday. That building houses classified historical records."

"Building 7 has restricted status," Jasper interjected. "Most records stored there were sealed after the Hayes file destruction orders were implemented."

"Exactly." Aria's finger traced a timeline. "Yet Harper possesses keycard access to what officially shouldn't be accessed. And her subsequent private meeting with you, Madam President, raises additional questions about her knowledge and activities."

Jordan studied the documentation, her mind cycling through prosecutorial considerations. "Under normal circumstances, I wouldn't authorize investigation of a political opponent based on this evidence. But given the potential national security implications—"

"You'd be crucified in the press," Finn warned.

"We need clarity on what Harper knows about Hayes's potential survival," Jordan decided. "Aria, initiate a limited inquiry. Financial records, communications analysis, travel patterns for the past five years."

"Understood. Though you should know—" Aria paused strategically, "—my preliminary research indicates Harper's sister Bella exhibited behaviors remarkably similar to Nina's current presentation. Right down to claiming Hayes spoke directly to her."

Jasper shifted uncomfortably. "Investigating mental health records crosses ethical boundaries."

"The files are already sealed," Aria countered. "But they were reviewed by federal agencies during Bella's initial psychiatric evaluation. The documented parallels are... significant."

The meeting concluded with a decision that felt simultaneously necessary and potentially disastrous. Jordan issued the investigation order with the specific caveat of potential obstruction of justice—Harper's presence near Nina shortly before the Hayes sighting warranted examination.

By midday, the investigation's first findings appeared on Jordan's desk. Aria delivered them personally, her expression carefully controlled.

"Bella Harper was admitted to Riverside Psychiatric fourteen months ago, diagnosed with severe PTSD and delusional disorder. The admission notes are extraordinary." She placed a printout before Jordan. "The patient exhibited abnormal knowledge of classified Purist operational details. She claimed Asher Hayes 'showed her things' that only intelligence operatives should know."

"Where is she now?"

"That's the problematic aspect." Aria's professional composure wavered slightly. "No one's seen her for eleven months. Her room's maintained as occupied, bills paid regularly, but staff report only brief glimpses—always from behind, in poor lighting."

The investigation broadened rapidly. By Wednesday, they'd traced Harper's financial history to a series of transactions that defied simple explanation: regular payments to a cemetery that hadn't existed for six years, donations to three charities that had dissolved before The Purists' emergence.

"She's covering tracks," Liam concluded during their morning session. "But what tracks?"

Aria presented additional findings. "Hospital staff interviews revealed Bella's obsession began after intercepting her father's correspondence about the Hayes trial. She started researching extensively, claimed she was 'meant to understand the truth.' Then she began displaying specific mannerisms—the same odd cadences and physical gestures Nina exhibits."

"The patient records indicate something else," Aria continued. "Bella experienced what doctors termed 'comprehensive historical recall'—she could detail events from Hayes's life that hadn't been publicly documented. When questioned, she insisted Hayes was speaking through her."

Jordan leaned back, processing implications. "And she disappeared."

"Or rather, someone else started paying her bills and simulating her presence."

The investigation leaked Thursday morning. Someone—Aria suspected a clerk in financial records—had disclosed the Harper inquiry to media contacts. By noon, Freedom Voice Network ran headlines questioning the administration's motives.

Finn burst into the Oval Office, his usual composure fractured.

"FVN is calling it a witch hunt. They're saying you're targeting political opponents. We need to get ahead of this—"

"Schedule a press conference," Jordan decided. "Tomorrow, 10 AM. We address it directly."

"What's our angle?"

"National security inquiry. Routine investigation following classified security breach." Jordan's prosecutorial instincts engaged. "We don't discuss specifics about Hayes or mental health. Just the official rationale."

"And if they ask about Bella Harper?"

"We protect her privacy while confirming investigations sometimes reveal concerning patterns."

The preparation consumed the afternoon. Jordan reviewed talking points while Aria compiled supporting documentation for any potential congressional inquiries. The weight of choosing this path pressed steadily against her resolve.

That evening, alone in the Oval Office, Jordan placed a call to the Riverside Psychiatric facility. As president, her request for information carried unprecedented weight. Dr. Marcus Reed, Chief of Psychiatry, was formally cooperative.

"I cannot discuss specific patients, Madam President, but I can confirm our security protocols are exemplary. Any concerns about patient whereabouts should be addressed through proper channels."

"This is national security related, Dr. Reed."

"Even so, patient confidentiality—"

"Have you personally seen Bella Harper recently?"

A pause. "Not... personally, no. But our staff—"

"What exactly have they seen?"

Another hesitation. "Glimpses. At night. Through windows. Her room shows signs of occupancy—moved objects, used bedding."

"Has anyone spoken with her face-to-face in the past year?"

"I'd need to review our logs thoroughly to—"

"I'll require those logs by morning, Dr. Reed. And complete staff interviews."

After disconnecting, Jordan drafted an executive order for Aria's expanded investigation. The document felt dangerous as she signed it—potentially career-ending. But the alternatives seemed worse.

Friday morning arrived with political pressure intensifying. The United Media Corporation reported Senator Harper's office denied any wrongdoing but acknowledged "standard government facilities access for congressional research purposes." The network speculated about Jordan's motives, suggesting desperation to distract from legislative challenges.

At 9:45 AM, as Jordan prepared for the press conference, Aria delivered one final revelation: "Hospital security footage shows something irregular. Bella's room has movement at night—shadows, shifting shapes. But when guards investigate, it's always empty."

"Someone's impersonating her?"

"Or maintaining the illusion of her presence for financial purposes."

Finn appeared at Jordan's office door. "Three minutes, Madam President. Are you certain about this path?"

Was she? The investigation had already damaged her political capital. But abandoning it now would signal guilty retreat. She remembered her oath from mere days ago—to preserve, protect, and defend.

"I'm ready."

The White House Press Room buzzed with anticipation. Finn introduced the President with unusual brevity, then stepped aside as Jordan approached the podium.

"Good morning. I'm here to address recent reports regarding an ongoing investigation." Her voice carried steady authority. "Following specific security breaches and unusual activities near sensitive government facilities, we've initiated inquiries that—as often happens—have expanded to include various individuals with potential information."

Hands shot up immediately.

"Nicole Martinez, Associated Post. Are you targeting political opponents?"

"I'm executing presidential responsibilities regarding national security. Political affiliation carries no weight in threat assessment."

"David Chen, Washington Inquirer. Can you comment on reports that you're investigating Senator Harper's family medical history?"

"Medical privacy remains sacred. Our investigation concerns potential security breaches and missing persons situations that intersected with government facilities."

"Susan Torres, UMC. Sources claim this relates to resurrected threats from The Purists era. Can you confirm?"

A loaded question. Jordan choose words precisely. "We're examining several cases where individuals claiming knowledge about historical threats may possess information relevant to current security concerns."

The press conference continued for thirty-seven minutes. Jordan deflected inquiries about specific targets, Bella Harper's whereabouts, and any connection to Nina Foster. She maintained professional composure while providing minimal confirmation of anything substantive.

As she concluded, Michael Torres from ABN pressed one final question: "Madam President, if this investigation proves fruitless, will you accept responsibility for potentially abusing executive power?"

"I accept responsibility for all decisions made in service of this nation's security. Thank you."

Later that evening, watching the cable news coverage from the residence, Jordan witnessed her political landscape shifting. Freedom Voice Network led with "President Prescott's Partisan Purge." United Media Corporation countered with "Breaking the Glass Ceiling Creates New Enemies." American Broadcasting Network displayed split-screen polls showing her approval ratings beginning a concerning descent.

Her secure phone vibrated. Aria: "Dr. Reed just called. Staff inspection of Bella's room revealed something unexpected. Hidden journal entries describing Hayes's 'return' with dates predicting significant events—your election among them."

Jordan responded: "Authentic handwriting?"

"Forensics confirms. But here's the issue: some entries describe events that haven't occurred yet."

In the residence's private study, Jordan reviewed the investigation's accumulated evidence. Patterns emerged—Bella and Nina sharing identical delusions, Harper's inexplicable activities, historical precedents suggesting something deeply wrong with Hayes's reported death.

Michael entered quietly, finding her surrounded by classified documents. "You look terrible."

"I've declared war on my own reputation." She rubbed her temples. "And I'm not certain anymore if I'm fighting monsters or windmills."

"What does your gut say?"

"That's the problem. My gut screams there's a genuine threat. But every prosecutor's instinct warns this evidence won't convince anyone—it'll just destroy us both."

The weekend brought a deluge of political commentary. Senator Bill Crawford called for Jordan's censure. Representative Maria Gonzalez defended the investigation's necessity. Evelyn Harper maintained dignified silence, which somehow made her appear more victimized.

By Sunday afternoon, Finn presented polling data showing Jordan's approval rating had dropped eight points in three days.

"We need to change the narrative."

"To what? That I might be right about investigating impossible threats?" Jordan's laugh sounded hollow. "The political cost is escalating daily. But stopping now admits either guilt or irresponsibility."

Aria entered with an update. "Bella's journal contained one more entry. Written yesterday." She handed Jordan a single page.

In precise handwriting: "Jordan will understand soon. Some truths require destruction to reveal themselves. Ask Nina about the recording. Ask her what she hears at night. The purification begins with truth."

Jordan read it three times, each reading deepening her unease. "This was written after her disappearance?"

"Hospital confirms the journal remained in her abandoned room. No one entered that space for months."

"Handwriting analysis?"

"Matches perfectly. Down to pressure variations and micro-tremors specific to Bella's previous samples."

The implications crashed over Jordan like momentum she couldn't arrest. Either multiple people were experiencing identical delusions with impossible elements, or something far more disturbing connected them across time and space.

Monday morning arrived with catastrophic political news. Three senators had drafted articles of inquiry regarding Jordan's investigation. The phrase "political witch hunt" dominated headlines. Her own party members were reportedly discussing distancing strategies.

In the Oval Office, Jordan faced her core team—Aria, Liam, and Finn.

"The National Observer is preparing an op-ed comparing this to

McCarthy-era paranoia," Finn reported grimly. "They have quotes from five constitutional scholars questioning your actions."

"Should we pull back from the Harper investigation?" Liam asked.

Jordan considered the accumulated evidence: Nina's impossible knowledge, Bella's predictive journal entries, Harper's mysterious activities, Jasper's unclear memories of the file destruction. Each element could be explained away individually. Together, they suggested something reality struggled to accommodate.

"No," she decided finally. "We pursue this to conclusion. But Aria—find Nina. We need answers about these recordings the journal mentioned."

Chapter Four

The Situation Room was empty except for Jordan and the secure phone linking her to Aria. Wednesday morning light filtered through the bulletproof windows as they discussed overnight surveillance findings.

"Harper met with three former intelligence operatives yesterday," Aria reported. "Two were forced into early retirement during the post-Hayes restructuring. They'd been investigating discrepancies in the death report."

"And now they're meeting privately with a senator who happens to access restricted archives?" Jordan pinched the bridge of her nose. "Schedule a meeting with Harper. This afternoon."

"Madam President?" Liam entered, looking frazzled. "There's a situation. Nina Foster accessed White House visitor logs from her school's computer lab—found out Senator Harper is scheduled here today. She's demanding to speak with you before the meeting."

"How did she—never mind. Have security bring her to the Roosevelt Room. Ten minutes only."

Nina arrived wearing her Trinity Prep blazer, but her carefully composed appearance couldn't hide trembling hands. She stood rather than sitting, energy crackling through her thin frame.

"I need to know what you've found about Senator Harper," she said without preamble.

"Nina, this is a presidential investigation—"

"She was near the orphanage. The same day." Nina's voice rose. "You think that's coincidence? She's connected somehow, maybe even helping him—"

"Enough." Jordan's prosecutor tone cut through the room. "You are fourteen years old. You've provided valuable information, and we're following every lead. But you are not part of this investigation."

"I started it!" Nina slammed her palm on the table. "Without me, you'd still think Hayes was dead. I deserve—"

"You deserve protection. And treatment if you need it." Jordan softened slightly. "I know this is personal for you. But letting you participate could compromise everything we're trying to accomplish."

"So I'm just supposed to go back to school? Pretend everything's normal while you dig around behind my back?"

"Yes." Jordan moved to the window, watching cars stream past the White House gates. "Sometimes the hardest thing we can do is trust others to handle situations beyond our control. Can you do that?"

Nina's shoulders slumped. "I guess I have to."

After she left, Jordan consulted her daily briefing papers, noting several legislative items requiring attention. One caught her eye—the Federal Database Access Act. She skimmed it quickly, her mind still on the confrontation with Nina: bureaucratic language about improving inter-agency cooperation, streamlining information sharing. Routine administrative stuff. Nina was really…different today. Even her voice sounded a bit different, a little edgier, like she wasn't…completely herself. She initialed her approval without reading the full text, completely distracted. She forced her mind to shift to the Harper meeting.

At 3:00 PM, Evelyn Harper entered the Oval Office with the bearing of someone preparing for battle. She declined tea, settling into a wingback chair across from Jordan's desk.

"This investigation is unconscionable," Harper began without pleasantries. "You're destroying careers based on a teenager's delusions."

"We're examining potential security breaches," Jordan replied calmly. "Your visits to restricted facilities require explanation."

"Congressional oversight. Which you'd know if you bothered checking proper protocols before sending federal agents to interview my staff."

"The protocols that allow you to access archives that officially don't exist?"

Harper's eyes narrowed. "You're playing with forces you don't understand. This isn't about Hayes, it's about maintaining the stability we worked decades to rebuild after his terror campaign."

"Explain that to Nina Foster. Explain why your office had a government vehicle near the orphanage minutes before Hayes allegedly reappeared."

"Coincidence. I support children's charities."

"With state vehicles?"

Harper stood abruptly. "You're so desperate to prove your competence, you're willing to resurrect national trauma? To target political rivals? This is exactly why some questioned whether a female president could handle pressure without becoming paranoid."

Jordan felt heat rise in her cheeks. "My gender is irrelevant to my qualifications."

"Then act like it. Stop chasing ghosts and address real issues. Unless you'd rather confirm every sexist stereotype about emotional decision-making."

"Get out of my office." The words came colder than intended.

"Gladly. But when this investigation crumbles—and it will—remember who warned you about the cost of paranoia." Harper paused at the door. "And read your legislation more carefully. You've just signed away more civil liberties than any administration since 1949."

Jordan opened her mouth to respond, but Harper had already swept from the room. The barb about legislation gnawed at her concentration. She buzzed her assistant. "Send me the full text of any bills I've approved today."

Thursday morning brought catastrophe. The Federal Database Access Act dominated headlines: "PRESIDENT PRESCOTT CREATES SURVEILLANCE STATE" screamed the Washington Monitor. Civil liberties groups issued scathing statements. The ACLU announced immediate court challenges.

"I thought it was routine administrative reform," Jordan protested as Finn delivered increasingly dire press summaries. "How did I miss this?"

"The bill's language was deliberately obscure," Liam explained, pulling up sections. "Look: 'facilitating cross-platform data synthesis' means warrantless access to private medical records. 'Streamlining identification protocols' allows facial recognition without oversight."

"Who drafted this?"

"Senator Crawford from the Conservative Covenant. He's been pushing surveillance expansion for years."

"And I just handed him everything he wanted." Jordan slumped in her chair. "Because I was distracted by chasing Hayes instead of doing my actual job."

Aria entered with additional bad news. "The press knows about Nina now. Someone leaked her identity to APB News. They're running a piece tonight questioning your mental fitness for office."

The investigation's political cost mounted hourly. By noon, three

Progressive Alliance senators had publicly distanced themselves from the administration. Senator Patricia Walsh, usually a reliable ally, told reporters she was "deeply concerned about the direction of presidential priorities."

Evelyn Harper remained pointedly silent, letting Jordan's mistakes speak for themselves.

Friday brought no relief. Freedom Voice Network launched a special series: "The Paranoid Presidency." Host Martin Davis opened his evening show with damning imagery: Jordan signing the privacy-destroying bill with one hand while pointing at imaginary threats with the other.

"We have sources indicating President Prescott is pursuing a vendetta against Senator Evelyn Harper based on the testimony of a disturbed teenager," Davis reported. "Meanwhile, Americans' fundamental rights were traded away without the President even reading the legislation she signed."

The investigation files grew thicker while Jordan's approval ratings plummeted. Surveillance teams found no evidence of Hayes activity at former Purist sites. Harper's financial records revealed charitable donations and legitimate consulting fees—nothing suspicious enough to justify federal scrutiny.

Aria presented her findings with characteristic efficiency. "Harper's meetings with ex-intelligence operatives appear focused on fact-gathering about the original Hayes investigation. They're building documentation about procedural failures during the crisis years—potentially for a memoir or historical project."

"Not planning an assassination or cover-up?"

"The evidence suggests legitimate historical research."

Jordan stared at the accumulating reports. Each page represented resources diverted from actual governance to pursue increasingly implausible theories. The woman who promised methodical, evidence-based leadership had become exactly what her critics predicted: emotional, paranoid, distracted by shadows.

"Madam President?" Aria's voice carried unusual hesitation. "There's one finding we should discuss privately."

After others left, Aria placed a single document on the desk. "We found this in Nina's school locker during a wellness check. It's dated next week."

Jordan read Nina's precise handwriting:

April 16: The President discovers the truth about the investigation. Harper's theory about possession proves partially correct. But it's not Hayes alone. The fragments spread wider than anyone imagined. Jordan will blame herself for the Database Act. She shouldn't. We're all being played.

"How can she write about events that haven't happened?" Jordan whispered.

"I don't know. But it suggests either extraordinary insight or..." Aria paused carefully.

"Or what?"

"Or she's experiencing something beyond our understanding."

The weekend arrived with Jordan isolated in mounting political disaster. The Senate judiciary committee scheduled hearings about the Database Act. Three lawsuits challenged its constitutionality. Editorial pages demanded Jordan stop "tilting at windmills" and focus on real issues.

Sunday evening, Jordan sat alone in the Oval Office, surrounded by investigation files that yielded nothing substantial while her presidency burned. She'd chased a ghost at Nina Foster's behest and managed to destroy her credibility, her approval rating, and potentially civil liberties for millions.

A knock interrupted her rumination. Finn entered cautiously. "Madam President? Senator Harper is here. Says it's urgent and cannot wait."

"I thought she was through with me."

"She seems different. Concerned rather than angry."

Harper entered looking haggard, her composure visibly strained. She sat without invitation, hands clasped tightly.

"I came to apologize," she said quietly. "And to share something I should have told you earlier."

"What's that?"

"My sister Bella... she predicted your election. Eighteen months ago, during her worst episode." Harper pulled out a crumpled paper. "She drew this map of Washington, marked specific buildings. Including a safe house we've been watching since Thursday."

Jordan studied the map, recognizing streets from Aria's surveillance reports.

"There's more." Harper's voice dropped. "The operatives I met with? They've been comparing notes. Multiple people across the country have experienced what they're calling 'Hayes events'—unexplained knowledge, predictive abilities, personality changes. Always related to that man."

"You're saying you believe Nina?"

"I'm saying I'm no longer certain what to believe. My sister took years to recover, with intensive therapy and isolation. Nina would need the same. But you can't disappear a teenage witness without political death."

"So I just surrender?"

"You prepare for managed transition. Theo Marshall is clean—we've monitored him extensively. You can hand off power gracefully, claiming medical leave. Continue protecting America from the shadows instead of being destroyed in public."

Jordan felt the weight of impossible choice. "How do I know I can trust you?"

Harper produced her phone, playing a recording. "Listen carefully."

A voice—unmistakably Asher Hayes—spoke through static: "The

girl's placement is confirmed. When the glass ceiling breaks, shards will injure the breakthrough. Victory through her descent."

"This recording was intercepted three years ago," Harper explained. "I've been preparing ever since. The supreme irony—he planned to destroy the first female president before one was even elected. You were targeted for breaking that barrier alone."

Outside, early morning commerce began on Pennsylvania Avenue. Inside, America's first female president contemplated a path that offered only variations of defeat: political destruction through investigation, or voluntary abdication to protect the nation.

"I need time," Jordan said finally.

"Time accelerates everything," Harper warned. "The investigation has already cost you the moderate voters. Another week, and you'll trigger the failsafe responses I've seen before—mass desertions, cabinet questioning competency. Hayes designed perfect political poison."

After Harper departed, Jordan remained in the residence, messaging Aria to compile complete files on every action taken since inauguration. Numbers told brutal truths: seventeen million spent, approval ratings in freefall, legislative agenda in chaos.

By noon, medical reports confirmed Nina's deteriorating condition was self-correcting—suggesting whatever Hayes had been implementing was reaching completion. The girl's original personality would likely return, carrying impossible knowledge that would mark her forever.

Liam found Jordan at the Resolute Desk, signing executive orders that consolidated power and prepared for potential transition.

"What's our plan?" he asked.

"Controlled burn," she replied. "We expose enough truth to prevent chaos but accept political consequences. Nina gets intensive psychiatric care. The investigation shifts focus to prevention rather than proving Hayes's existence."

"And Harper?"

"Remains publicly opposed while privately assisting transition. Democracy needs functioning opposition, even artificial ones."

As evening approached, Jordan prepared her address to the nation. She would acknowledge investigation costs, accept responsibility for the Database Act, announce medical evaluation at advisor requests.

The girl who broke the highest glass ceiling would be remembered as the first to discover what lurked in its shadow.

Chapter Five

The crack of splintering wood echoed through the Montana woods as Aria Collins kicked in the cabin door. Her tactical gear was soaked through from three hours of crawling through wet underbrush, but her Glock remained steady in her hand.

"Levi Parker! Federal agents! Come out with your hands visible!"

Silence answered, broken only by rain drumming on the corrugated tin roof. Aria signaled her team forward. Thirteen years of tracking—thirteen years since Asher Hayes's reported death—had led to this rotting cabin thirty miles from the Canadian border.

Agent Martinez moved to her left, weapon trained on the dark interior. "Collins, we've got movement—"

The bullet caught Martinez in the shoulder, spinning him backward. Aria dove through the doorway as gunfire erupted from the cabin's depths. Wood chips and dust rained down as her team returned fire.

"Parker's a dead man," growled Agent Hammond, pressing forward.

"No!" Aria barked. "I need him alive!"

Through the chaos, she glimpsed a figure moving between rooms—tall, lean, still quick despite nearly a decade and a half since his last confirmed sighting. The cabin's layout was familiar from surveillance photos: main room, two bedrooms, root cellar. Everywhere a man might hide.

Parker had prepared well. The walls revealed hidden reinforcements as bullets embedded into steel plating instead of wood. A flash-bang detonated in the corner, temporarily blinding Agent Chen. The cabin's windows had been sealed shut, turning the structure into an armored box.

"Collins!" Hammond shouted. "He's making for the back—"

Aria was already moving. Years of training took over as she flowed through the cabin's defenses. Parker had placed trip wires across doorways, but she'd studied his patterns. His left-handed preference meant he'd favor certain angles. His old shoulder injury would limit his mobility.

She found him in the bathroom, attempting to pry boards from a back window. When he spun to face her, Aria saw time had not been kind. Gray streaked through hair that had once been purely black. Scars crisscrossed hands that still gripped his weapon with deadly familiarity.

"Stand down, Parker," she ordered. "It's over."

His laugh was harsh. "For you, maybe. But not for him. Never for him."

The shot came faster than expected. Aria felt the bullet whistle past her ear as she dropped low, returning fire. Parker's next shot went wide— his old injury finally showing—and Aria put two rounds center mass.

But Parker wasn't finished. As he fell, he grabbed a hidden cord. The cabin's floor beneath them gave way as a prepared trapdoor opened. Both agents plummeted into darkness.

They landed hard on packed earth eight feet below. Parker recovered first, his familiarity with the space giving him advantage. He struck out with a combat knife that appeared from nowhere, forcing Aria to parry with her forearm.

Pain shot through her arm—the blade was serrated—but she maintained her grip on her weapon. Parker was strong, but decades of living rough had taken their toll. His movements, while skilled, lacked the precision of his prime.

They grappled in the cramped space. Parker's fingers sought her throat as she struggled to bring her gun to bear. Through gritted teeth, he spoke: "You people never understood. Hayes was more than a man. More than idea. He is transformation itself."

Aria headbutted him, feeling his nose crunch against her skull. As he recoiled, she finally got leverage, driving her knee into his stomach. The wind left him in a rush, and she pressed her advantage, hammering the butt of her weapon against his temple until he slumped unconscious.

Footsteps above indicated her team approaching. "Collins!" Hammond called down. "You alive?"

"Barely," she rasped. "Get medical down here. Martinez needs attention, and I need this bastard secured for transport."

As paramedics descended to treat her wounded arm, Aria studied Parker's unconscious form. Thirteen years of hunting, hundreds of leads, countless dead ends—all culminating in this moment. But holding the enemy felt different than expecting him. Parker seemed smaller somehow, more human than the shadow she'd been chasing.

Yet his words lingered: "He is transformation itself."

Three hours later, Aria stood in a secure transport vehicle as it wound its way toward a CIA black site near Missoula. Parker remained sedated, restrained, under constant watch. Her arm throbbed beneath professional bandaging, Martinez was in stable condition at a local hospital, and the team had secured enough evidence from the cabin to fill two vehicles.

But success felt hollow as she considered what came next. Thirteen years of her life dedicated to this pursuit, and now she had to extract information from a man who'd spent equally long avoiding this exact situation.

The secure phone buzzing against her chest interrupted dark thoughts. Only one person had this number.

"Aria," Jordan's voice carried both relief and concern. "The Montana team reported success. Casualties?"

"Martinez took a round to the shoulder. Flesh wound. I've got a knife cut that'll need attention. Parker's secure."

"And his condition?"

Aria glanced at the sedated prisoner. "Physically declining but mentally sharp. We found evidence he's been reaching out to old contacts. Letters, coded messages. He's still in the network."

"Bring him in quietly. No law enforcement, no federal custody. I need this invisible."

"Understood." Aria hesitated. "There's something else. When I captured him, he said Hayes 'is transformation itself.' What the hell does that mean?"

Static crackling suggested Jordan had moved to a more secure location. "We'll discuss it when you return. The forensics team has findings on Nina's evidence. Nothing's adding up the way we hoped."

"Meaning?"

"Meaning hurry back. We need answers, and Parker might be our last chance to get them without destroying everything I've built here."

The call ended abruptly. Aria leaned back against cold metal, contemplating the mission's parameters. No law enforcement meant they'd operate in a legal gray area. No federal custody suggested interrogation methods that couldn't be officially sanctioned.

Her training prepared her for such situations. CIA had protocols for extracting information when national security demanded extraordinary measures. But this felt different. The investigation had consumed Jordan's presidency, turned allies into enemies, and now demanded Aria cross lines she'd only theoretically considered.

Parker stirred slightly, sedation wearing thin. Aria watched his eyelids flutter, considering approaches. Physical coercion had its limits—pushing too hard risked fabrication or shock-induced memory loss. But psychological pressure, combined with measured pain, often yielded results.

The vehicle turned off paved road onto a dirt track. Twenty more minutes to the facility. Twenty minutes to prepare herself for what came next.

When they arrived, Aria coordinated Parker's transfer to an isolated wing. The facility—officially a forestry research station—maintained sophisticated interrogation capabilities. Soundproof rooms, medical monitoring, recording equipment that captured micro-expressions and stress indicators.

By 10:00 PM Eastern, Aria stood in a sterile observation room, watching Parker through one-way glass. He'd been secured to a medical examination chair, his wrists and ankles restrained but circulation maintained. Optimal for extended sessions.

Dr. Elena Reeves, the psychologist from Task Force Ghost, joined her. "He's fully conscious now. Vitals are strong despite his age. The medical team reports chronic joint damage consistent with extended outdoor survival."

"His pain threshold?"

"Based on field behavior and medical scans, considerably high. Standard interrogation techniques may prove ineffective."

Aria studied Parker's face—weathered but alert, eyes constantly scanning his surroundings. Thirteen years of evading the world's most sophisticated intelligence agencies required more than physical endurance.

"We start with conversation," she decided. "Establish baseline, probe for emotional triggers."

Dr. Reeves nodded. "I'll monitor from here. Watch for truth indicators versus performance."

Aria entered the interrogation room carrying two bottles of water and a medical report. Parker tracked her movement but remained silent as she settled across from him.

"You're looking well, considering," she began conversationally. "Montana wilderness is harsh this time of year."

Parker's smile revealed dental work—amateur but functional. "Better than federal prison."

"About that. We're not federal. No lawyers, no rights, no witnesses. Just you and me and time to spare."

"Then kill me and be done with it."

Aria sipped her water, studying his micro-expressions. "Death ends secrets. I prefer living sources."

"You'll get nothing from me."

"Everyone says that initially." She placed the medical report on the table. "Your hands tell stories. Six untreated fractures, old knife wounds, what appears to be a badly healed gunshot from... December 2000? Just months after Hayes's reported death."

Parker's jaw tightened almost imperceptibly.

"Interesting timing," Aria continued. "Sources indicate you were shot by former associates while trying to leave the movement. They buried you in a shallow grave in Oregon. Yet here you are."

"Stories have multiple versions."

"Indeed. For instance, the story of Asher Hayes's death. Multiple witnesses, security footage, positive identification. Yet here we are, chasing shadows because a child claims to have seen him."

"Children see many things."

"Nina Foster saw you," Aria said sharply. "Near her orphanage.

Three blocks from where she encountered Hayes. Coincidence?"

"Everything's coincidence when you're looking for patterns."

Aria leaned forward. "We found your correspondence in the cabin. Coded letters to known Purist sympathizers. You were rebuilding the network."

"I was helping survivors. Former members trying to rebuild lives after your people destroyed them."

"By planning what? Another reign of terror?"

Parker's silence stretched. Aria noted increased blood pressure on the monitors, elevated breathing rate. She'd struck something.

"Let's talk about Hayes's abilities," she shifted. "You were his closest advisor. If anyone understood what he could do..."

"What he could do?" Parker laughed. "You have no comprehension."

"Educate me."

"Why? So you can weaponize it? Create your own army of transformed beings?"

"So we can defend against it. Unless you'd prefer he continues unchecked."

Parker studied her for long moments. "You truly believe he's alive."

"Evidence suggests it."

"Evidence can deceive. Perception shapes reality. These were his favorite concepts."

Aria felt they were approaching something crucial. "Explain."

"Asher didn't see people as fixed entities. He understood human consciousness is malleable. Memories can transfer. Personalities can merge. What you call 'death' is merely transition between vessels."

The room seemed colder suddenly. "Possession?"

"Crude term. Think of it as... shared existence. The host retains agency but gains additional awareness. Memories. Abilities."

"And he could do this at will?"

Parker nodded slowly. "With proper preparation. Physical contact. Emotional connection. It's why he targeted children—their consciousnesses are still forming, more receptive to integration."

Aria processed this, implications cascading. "Nina Foster."

"Perhaps. Or she could be experiencing residual effects. Even killing the primary vessel doesn't always sever connections."

"How do we stop it?"

"You don't stop transformation. You can only try to understand it."

Aria stood, frustration mounting. Two hours of careful questioning had yielded hints but no concrete answers. Parker seemed willing to philosophize but not provide actionable intelligence. She signaled Dr. Reeves, who entered with sedatives and medical equipment.

"We're going to try something different," Aria announced. "Your pain threshold is admirable. Let's test its limits."

"Torture yields false information," Parker stated calmly.

"Not when applied correctly." Aria nodded to the doctor, who prepared a syringe. "This is a muscle relaxant. Combined with precise pressure on nerve clusters, it creates intense sensation without permanent damage."

"You're better than this."

"I'm exactly what this situation requires."

The injection took effect quickly. Aria began with Parker's left hand—the less damaged one. She isolated the pinky finger, applying steady pressure to the knuckle joint.

"Let's start simple. How does Hayes choose vessels?"

Parker's breathing quickened but he remained silent.

Aria increased pressure. The finger began to bend backward beyond its natural range.

"Affinity," Parker gasped. "Emotional resonance. Loss creates vulnerability."

"Elaborate."

"Trauma opens doors in the mind. Grief. Rage. Fear. He flows through cracks in the psyche."

The finger dislocated with an audible pop. Parker's body convulsed against restraints, but no scream emerged.

"Which of your old associates remains active?"

"Most... scattered. Hiding."

"Names."

"They trusted me. I won't—"

Another finger snapped. Parker's eyes rolled back briefly before training reclaimed control.

"I can continue this for hours," Aria stated. "Or you can help us stop him."

"Stopping him... means understanding. Understanding him... changes you."

"I'll take that risk."

"Will you?" Parker's voice strained through pain. "Already he's affected you. This brutality? Not who you were thirteen years ago."

Aria paused, his words cutting unexpectedly. She reviewed her actions—would she have tortured a prisoner before obsessively hunting Hayes? The line between necessity and corruption blurred.

She repositioned for the third finger.

"Victor Caine," Parker blurted. "Former cell leader. Boston area. He's been... protecting himself. Creating wards."

"Wards against what?"

"Against possession. Requires specific materials. Silver. Holy water. Sounds like superstition but—"

"But it works," Aria finished. "How do you know?"

"Because I'm using them. How do you think I've avoided him this long?"

Dr. Reeves documented everything meticulously. Aria continued the session, extracting details about Purist traditions, warning signs of possession, potential ways to force Hayes from a host. By midnight, Parker had provided names, locations, and methodologies—enough intelligence to redirect the investigation entirely. His condition remained stable despite trauma, though psychological damage would take longer to assess.

"One final question," Aria said as medical staff prepared him for transport. "Nina Foster. If Hayes has possessed her, can she be saved?"

Parker met her gaze, something like pity in his eyes. "Everyone touched by him changes, agent. The question isn't saving her. It's whether you'll recognize what emerges."

Back in the observation room, Aria updated her secure files. Evidence photos, recorded confessions, new lead directions—the investigation had pivoted from chasing rumors to tracking an active supernatural threat.

Her phone buzzed: Jordan requesting immediate video conference upon return to DC.

As dawn broke over Montana mountains, Aria prepared for transport. Thirteen years hunting a ghost had yielded a monster far worse than initial intelligence suggested. And somewhere in Washington, Nina

Foster carried secrets that might destroy them all.

The flight back east would take eight hours. Aria spent them reviewing interrogation transcripts, considering implications, and wondering how to present Parker's revelations without sounding delusional.

Hayes wasn't just alive—he was actively searching for new vessels. And according to Parker, the closer they came to finding him, the more aggressively he'd act to preserve himself.

As her plane descended toward Andrews Air Force Base, Aria's phone showed multiple missed calls from the White House. Whatever forensics had discovered about Nina's evidence had apparently accelerated their timeline.

The hunt was no longer theoretical. And Aria suspected the prey had been watching them all along.

Jordan paced the Oval Office, secure tablets displaying forensics reports that shattered her remaining confidence. When Aria finally arrived—arm bandaged, exhaustion evident—the full weight of their situation crystallized.

"The button's fake," she stated without preamble. "High-quality reproduction of original Purist insignia, but manufactured within the last month."

Aria set down her field report. "Meaning someone's deliberately recreating them."

"Or planting evidence." Jordan continued pacing. "The photo's more concerning. Metadata shows it was taken correctly, but the car's license plate appears in our modified format—the system that didn't exist until this year."

"Parker confirmed Hayes can possess hosts," Aria reported. "Transfer consciousness, share memories. The human host retains physical control but gains his awareness."

Jordan stopped mid-stride. "So Nina could be—"

"Potentially. Or receiving influence without full possession. Parker described it as degrees of integration."

"How do we know Parker's telling the truth?"

"His specific details aligned with documented cases from Ghost files. He provided locations of protective wards, named current Purist sympathizers. Either he's the world's most prepared liar, or he's genuinely terrified of Hayes."

Jordan absorbed this, political ramifications warring with security concerns. "What about Nina herself? If she presented false evidence, could she be working against us?"

"Or being manipulated into it. Planting seeds of doubt about her credibility while simultaneously directing our investigation."

"Toward what end?"

"Perhaps misdirection. While we chase his former associates, Hayes operates elsewhere."

Jordan reviewed the forensics documents again. "We can't confront Nina directly. If she's possessed, we'd alert him. If she's not, we'd destroy a vulnerable teenager."

"Parker suggested protection methods. Specific materials that create barriers against possession."

"We implement them quietly. Nina receives enhanced security personnel wearing silver, carrying blessed items. Monitor her reactions."

Aria nodded. "Meanwhile, we pursue Parker's intelligence. Victor Caine in Boston. Others he named."

"Carefully. If we spook them, we lose potential sources."

"And the political situation?"

Jordan's laugh held no humor. "The Database Act has Congress demanding oversight hearings. My approval rating dropped another six points overnight. Harper's office leaked that her vehicle records were accessed—making us look vindictive."

"So we're racing against political collapse as much as physical threat."

"Exactly." Jordan returned to her desk, decision crystallizing. "We need a win. Something concrete. No more shadows or theories."

Aria opened her tablet. "Parker's revealed confession could suffice. On record admission from Hayes's former second-in-command about possession capabilities."

"Along with my admission that we tortured for information? That video would destroy us."

"Then we find another angle. Medical documentation exists about children exhibiting possession characteristics. Hospital records, psychiatric evaluations. Build circumstantial case about patterns."

Jordan considered this approach. "And if Nina's evidence continues deteriorating? If public realizes we've chased fabrications?"

"We adjust narrative. Hayes isn't just alive—he's actively manipulating American politics. Creating disinformation to destabilize government."

"You're suggesting we sell conspiracy theories to save face?"

"I'm suggesting we prepare for the possibility that conspiracy theories are actually facts."

The irony cut deeply. Jordan had built her career on evidence-based conclusions. Now faced with potential supernatural infiltration of the highest levels of government.

Aria's phone vibrated insistently. She checked, expression darkening. "Regional surveillance just reported unusual activity at the original Purist compound in Virginia. Movement inside a building that's been sealed since 2001."

"Could be squatters."

"Thermal signatures show multiple figures moving with military precision. And the security cameras we placed are displaying the same corruption pattern from the day of Hayes's supposed death."

Jordan felt destiny's weight settling firmly. Every path forward carried enormous risk. But inaction guaranteed Hayes would continue operating unchecked.

"Gather a team. Minimal force, maximum observation. I want to know what's in that compound."

"And if we find something?"

"Document everything. Multiple backups. We build cases not on theories but irrefutable evidence."

After Aria departed, Jordan returned to the windows. Washington continued its eternal rhythm as her mind processed impossibilities now feeling increasingly probable. Somewhere in the city, Nina Foster carried either a dangerous truth or dangerous delusions. Former Purists sympathizers potentially harbored a monster that transcended death itself. Her presidency—history's first female executive—had devolved into defending reality itself against supernatural intrusion. The irony would have been amusing if the stakes weren't existential.

A knock interrupted her rumination. Liam entered tentatively. "Madam President? The Senate Judiciary Committee needs preliminary responses about the Database Act by tomorrow. And CNN is reporting leaked details about the investigation into Harper."

"How detailed?"

"That we're examining her vehicle records. That Nina Foster's connected. That you've diverted resources from national priorities to chase conspiracy theories."

"Accurate then."

Liam approached carefully. "What aren't you telling me? This obsession with Hayes doesn't match the leader I've known for twenty years."

Jordan contemplated her friend. Liam had earned truth through decades of support. But exposing him to this reality—to actual supernatural threats—seemed both unfair and dangerous.

"I'm telling you to trust me. For now." She straightened. "Draft responses for Judiciary emphasizing national security priorities. Set up private meetings with key senators. And find out who's leaking information to CNN."

"And while you chase ghosts?"

"While I protect this country from threats you can't begin to imagine."

Liam withdrew, clearly unsatisfied. Jordan's isolation deepened with each concealed truth. Friends became potential security risks. Allies required careful compartmentalization. The presidency had transformed into a barrier against forces that would sound delusional if spoken aloud.

Her secure phone displayed a new message from Aria: "Virginia compound confirmed active. Requesting permission to breach."

Jordan's fingers hovered over the keyboard. Each authorization pushed them deeper into a one-way road where evidence and reality bent to accommodate impossible truths. She typed: "Proceed with caution. Document everything. This ends tonight one way or another."

Chapter Six

The evaluation report arrived on Jordan's desk at dawn. She'd authorized the comprehensive psychological assessment of Nina Foster two days ago, despite knowing it would leak and become political ammunition. Now, reading through twenty-three pages of clinical observations, she felt her grip on reality further slipping.

"Madam President?" Aria stood at the door, her bandaged arm a reminder of recent violence. "The evaluation results?"

"Disturbing." Jordan motioned her closer. "Dr. Reeves notes oppositional defiant disorder, possible conduct disorder. But listen to this: 'Subject exhibits advanced knowledge of historical events she shouldn't have access to. When shown a photo of a former Purist cell member, she correctly identified his role without any context.'"

"That could be explained by her obsession."

"Could it?" Jordan flipped to another page. "She drew a detailed map of a Purist training compound in Maryland. One that was never publicly documented. Described its layout down to secret passages our intelligence teams only discovered last year."

Aria took the report, scanning quickly. "The bullying incidents are... specific."

"Three victims. All matching Hayes's 'purity' criteria. She told one girl her father would 'join the impure soon.' That girl's father had undiagnosed cancer. Died two months later."

"Predictive knowledge isn't possession," Aria said carefully. "It's just... unsettling."

"Unsettling?" Jordan laughed without humor. "Her therapist reported violent outbursts where her voice changes. She writes with her non-dominant hand during these episodes. The handwriting matches Levi Parker's."

Aria set the report down. "Or she's traumatized and obsessive. Both explanations fit."

"That's the problem. Every symptom supports multiple theories." Jordan moved to the window. "Her teachers described her as manipulative. Charming to adults, terrifying to peers. Classic behavioral patterns."

"For troubled children."

"Or vessels."

The room settled into uncomfortable silence. Outside, protestors gathered—Database Act demonstrations had become daily occurrences. Signs reading "PRESCOTT'S POLICE STATE" competed with others calling her leadership weak, distracted.

"I need you to investigate her background deeper," Jordan decided. "Interview everyone who knew her. Teachers, foster families before the orphanage, medical records."

"That will definitely leak."

"Everything leaks." Jordan returned to her desk. "Meanwhile, Levi's claims about shapeshifting need verification. Establish surveillance on people he named as former associates."

"We're already monitoring Victor Caine in Boston."

"Expand it. And that Virginia compound—any updates?"

"Thermal imaging shows continued activity. Non-human heat signatures detected."

Jordan frowned. "Meaning?"

"Animals. Or..." Aria hesitated. "Or entities that don't register as human body temperature."

"Wonderful. Schedule the compound raid for tonight. Minimal force, maximum documentation."

After Aria left, Jordan reviewed additional psychological reports. One section particularly troubled her:

Subject claims to experience 'blackouts' where she loses time. During these episodes, classmates report personality changes. She becomes articulate, knowledgeable about topics beyond her education level. One teacher noted her discussing quantum physics concepts during a dissociative state.

When asked about these blackouts, subject becomes agitated. States: "Someone else is driving. I'm just watching."

The terminology felt familiar. Hayes's former manifesto referenced human consciousness as "vehicles to be driven." If Nina was possessed, how much remained of the original girl?

Her morning meeting with Liam brought no relief.

"The media has Bella Harper's disappearance," he reported grimly. "APB News ran a piece linking her to Nina. They're calling it 'The President's Pattern of Investigating Troubled Women.'"

"Sexism or legitimate concern?"

"Both." Liam placed newspapers across her desk. "But here's the interesting part. Bella's former psychology professor contacted me. Said he had concerns about his former student that he'd never shared with authorities."

"Why not?"

"Fear. Apparently she once described Hayes's compound layouts with perfect accuracy. Recalled conversations he'd never documented. The professor believed she'd somehow accessed classified files, but couldn't prove it."

Jordan contemplated the pattern. Multiple women, different generations, displaying impossible knowledge. Either an elaborate fraud spanning decades, or something far worse.

"Schedule me with Finn," she decided. "We need to control this narrative before it controls us."

That afternoon brought concerning news from the field. Agent Chen, still embedded at Nina's school as guidance counselor, reported escalating behavior.

"She attacked a janitor during lunch period," Chen detailed via secure call. "The man bumped her accidentally. Nina turned and hit him with such force that she dislocated his jaw. Four teachers had to restrain her."

"What triggered it?"

"The janitor wore a red bandana."

Jordan felt ice form in her stomach. Red had been The Purists' signature color. "How did she respond after?"

"That's the strange part. She immediately broke down crying, saying she didn't know what came over her. Seemed genuinely remorseful."

"Or performing remorse."

"Or switched back to being herself," Chen suggested carefully.

The distinction haunted Jordan through her afternoon briefings. Reality and deception blended until determining truth felt impossible. By evening, as she prepared for Aria's raid report, she found herself questioning her own perceptions.

The compound operation commenced at midnight. Jordan watched real-time feeds from the Situation Room, Aria's team moving with practiced precision through deteriorating buildings. Motion sensors detected movement. Thermal imaging confirmed non-standard heat signatures. But nothing could explain what cameras captured next.

"Recording devices are corrupting," Aria reported. "Same pattern as Hayes's death footage."

"Force entry. Document everything."

Twenty minutes of silence followed. When communication resumed, Aria's voice carried unprecedented strain. "Compound clear. But, Madam President... you need to see what we found."

The photographs arrived encrypted, requiring presidential clearance to view. Jordan's hands trembled slightly as she opened them.

Room after room showed evidence of recent occupation. Maps on walls detailed current government facilities—including the White House. Photographs of high-ranking officials, including Jordan herself, were pinned with notes describing their daily routines. But the most disturbing discovery dominated the final images.

A shrine. Dozens of photographs arranged in concentric circles—Bella Harper at the center, Nina Foster beside her, surrounded by images of other young women. Each photo bore red annotations: dates, times, locations. Some described the subjects as "vessels in waiting." Others noted "purification progress."

Beneath the shrine lay journals. Page after page of identical handwriting describing possession techniques, listing potential targets, detailing weaknesses in current security protocols. Multiple books, supposedly written years apart, all in the same precise script.

The final photograph showed a mirror inscribed with words that shouldn't have existed yet.

January 20, 2013: The glass ceiling shatters. New vessel established. The purification enters its final phase.

Jordan stared at her own inauguration date, written years before her candidacy was announced. Reality fractured further around impossible evidence.

"Secure everything," she commanded Aria. "Complete documentation lockdown. This information doesn't leave the compound."

"Understood. But the journals contain more. Specific names of people Hayes plans to inhabit. Including..." Aria paused. "Including several members of your staff."

Jordan closed her eyes against mounting implications. Her own team could be compromised. The investigation into Nina might itself be part of Hayes's manipulation. Every ally became potential enemy.

"Hold position. I'm dispatching a secondary team for extraction."

As she ended the call, her secure phone buzzed. Liam. She ignored it, knowing any conversation now would require careful calibration to avoid exposing what they'd discovered.

The internal message system showed priority notifications. Finn reporting more leaks. Chen updating about Nina's suspension from school. The Senate Judiciary Committee demanding expedited hearings about the Database Act.

Jordan reached for the scotch she'd been avoiding, pouring three fingers worth. Her campaign promises of transparent, ethical governance seemed darkly ironic now. The first female president was secretly battling supernatural possession while publicly defending politically disastrous decisions.

Her phone wouldn't stop buzzing. Messages accumulated about the Judiciary Committee, about international developments requiring attention, about the economy showing stress indicators. Normal presidential concerns competed with abnormal realities for attention.

Finally, she answered Liam's latest call.

"Where are you?" His voice carried an edge she recognized—suspicion masked as concern.

"Situation Room. Monitoring developments."

"What developments? You've been there eight hours."

"Classified briefings."

"Jordan." He used her first name deliberately. "Twenty years of friendship. I can tell when you're deflecting. This isn't about Nina Foster anymore, is it?"

"I can't—"

"People are noticing your isolation. Staff whispers about extended meetings, unexplained security measures. Your own cabinet questions your focus."

"My focus remains on national security."

"Or paranoia." The word hung sharp between them. "Remember what happened to Bella Harper. Isolation. Obsession. Seeing patterns where none existed."

"Or where they're deliberately hidden."

"Listen to yourself. You sound exactly like the conspiracy theorists we used to mock."

Jordan felt the familiar sting of doubt penetrating her resolve. How many times had she prosecuted cases where suspects claimed elaborate plots against them? When did justified caution become delusional paranoia?

"I need you to trust me," she said quietly. "A little longer."

"How long until you've sacrificed your presidency chasing shadows?"

After Liam disconnected, Jordan reviewed the day's developments. Each piece of evidence cut both ways—confirming suspicions while simultaneously suggesting elaborate delusion. The reports from Nina's evaluation particularly challenged comprehension.

Written by Dr. Sarah Mendez, Child Psychiatrist:

Subject exhibits symptoms consistent with complex PTSD following early childhood trauma. Blackouts and personality changes align with dissociative identity disorder presentation. However, the specificity of her "alternate" knowledge cannot be explained through conventional psychological frameworks.

Most concerning: During hypnosis session, subject spoke in voice not her own, referencing events from before her birth with verifiable accuracy. She described building layouts never publicly documented. Named people she couldn't have known.

Professional assessment: Either this child possesses extraordinary research capabilities and is engaging in elaborate performance, or she's experiencing something beyond current medical understanding.

Jordan highlighted the final sentence, the clinical language barely containing the doctor's uncertainty. Modern medicine struggled to accommodate supernatural possibilities, even when confronted with them directly.

The compound photographs haunted her peripheral vision. Hayes's careful documentation suggested planning extending back years, potentially decades. If possession worked as Levi described, how many people might already be compromised? Government officials? Military leadership? Her own staff?

Her office door opened without announcement. Theo Marshall, her Vice President, entered with his characteristic easy charm diminished by evident concern.

"Madam President. We need to discuss the state of your administration."

"Meaning?"

"Meaning your approval rating hit twenty-seven percent. Congressional support evaporates hourly. Three major newspapers are preparing pieces questioning your mental fitness for office."

"Based on?"

"Based on observable behavior. Extended isolation. Obsession with fringe theories. Diversion of resources to chase conspiracy theories about dead terrorists."

Theo sat without invitation. "I supported you becoming the first female president. Believe in your capabilities completely. But leadership requires acknowledging when you're wrong. The Database Act alone might not be survivable politically."

"What if I told you there's more to this investigation than appears publicly?"

"I'd ask for concrete evidence. Something beyond a teenager's testimony and elderly man's claims. Your presidency deserves better than to end in paranoid speculation."

Jordan studied her Vice President, trying to discern whether genuine concern or ambition motivated his intervention. The compound's mirror had named him as neither possessed nor target—a designation feeling increasingly irrelevant as reality shifted.

"Give me until week's end," she requested. "If the current investigations yield nothing substantive, I'll redirect resources to conventional governance."

"And if they yield more conspiracy theories?"

"Then we'll address my administration's viability. Together."

Theo departed with reluctant acceptance, leaving Jordan to contemplate her dwindling timeline. Five days to either prove an impossible reality or accept that her presidency had been destroyed by delusion.

The evening security briefing brought mixed developments. Virginia compound surveillance confirmed complete site abandonment following the raid. DNA analysis of found materials remained inconclusive—multiple subjects, some unidentifiable, suggesting Hayes's claimed shapeshifting capabilities might hold truth.

Aria reported additional findings from seized journals: "Detailed infiltration timeline spanning thirty years. Names of possessed individuals throughout government history, complete with handover protocols when hosts aged. Backup vessels identified for critical positions."

"Anyone currently active?"

"Journal suggests two confirmed possessions ongoing. No names provided, only positional references: 'The Shield' and 'The Vessel.'"

Jordan felt paranoia bloom. Her entire staff could be compromised. Every ally might harbor Hayes's consciousness.

"Increase surveillance on all senior administration officials. Discrete monitoring only."

"Including Vice President Marshall?"

"Especially him. But carefully. Very carefully."

That night, unable to sleep, Jordan reviewed accumulated evidence against encroaching sanity questions. The pattern seemed clear: Hayes had survived death, possessed multiple individuals, infiltrated the highest levels of government. Yet presenting this theory publicly guaranteed political destruction.

Her secure line buzzed at 3:00 AM. Aria again. "Madam President. We've intercepted communications suggesting another abduction attempt on Nina."

"When?"

"Within forty-eight hours. Source indicates Hayes plans to fully integrate Nina's consciousness before we can extract useful information."

"How is this possible? We have her under complete protection."

"The source suggests inside assistance. Someone on her protection detail may be compromised."

Jordan's mind raced through options. Confront Nina directly about her past behavior, the disturbing reports, and risk alerting Hayes to their knowledge. Maintain current course and possibly lose their only direct connection to the truth. Or take unprecedented action to secure Nina's consciousness before it became fully Hayes's domain.

"Implement medical intervention protocols," she decided. "Full sedation. Psychiatric specialists only. Begin documenting everything that emerges during controlled consciousness separation."

"Madam President," Aria hesitated. "That's essentially kidnapping and medical experimentation on a minor."

"It's protecting national security."

"It's what we'd condemn authoritarian regimes for doing."

The irony cut deeply. In pursuing protection against tyranny, Jordan was implementing tyrannical methods. The moral boundaries of her office blurred against existential threats.

"Make it happen. Quietly."

By Saturday morning, covert medical teams had transported Nina to a secure facility. The operation remained unknown to all but essential personnel. Yet Jordan felt the gravity of crossing this threshold—from constitutional president to authoritarian guardian against occult threats.

The research commenced as political pressure intensified. Senate hearings were announced. Media speculation about Jordan's stability reached fever pitch. Meanwhile, doctors attempted to separate demonic influence from damaged child, reality from delusion.

The psychological evaluation's final reports arrived as Washington buzzed with rumors of administrative crisis:

Nina Foster exhibits definitive signs of dissociative identity disorder with highly unusual presentations. Secondary personality demonstrates knowledge impossible for her to acquire through normal means. Hypnotic regression reveals memories predating her birth, including detailed accounts of Asher Hayes's operations.

Most significantly: When sedated, subject speaks in multiple distinct voices, referencing contemporaneous events across different decades. Brain scans during these episodes show activity patterns inconsistent with current neurological understanding.

Clinical assessment pending additional testing, but preliminary finding suggests subject may be experiencing something beyond conventional psychiatric explanation.

Jordan highlighted the carefully worded conclusion—doctors unable to fully embrace possession theory yet unable to dismiss accumulated evidence. Science struggled against boundaries reality insisted on transcending.

Chapter Seven

The Senate Judiciary Committee chamber felt smaller than Liam remembered, somehow narrowed by the weight of circumstances. As Executive Assistant to the President, he'd testified before, but never like this—never with cameras documenting his every micro-expression, never with his twenty-year friendship on trial alongside the Database Act.

Senator Patricia Walsh gaveled the hearing to order at precisely 9:00 AM. The committee chair's face bore the carefully practiced neutrality of someone who'd already decided the verdict.

"Today's hearing concerns the Federal Database Access Act and its implementation," Walsh announced. "We'll begin with testimony from Executive Assistant Liam Bennett."

The opening questions established what everyone already knew— the Act had been signed without proper review. But as the morning progressed, the inquiry sharpened.

"Mr. Bennett," Senator Torres began, spreading documents across her desk, "we have reports that the Database Act has already been used to access medical records of 847 citizens, financial data of 1,291 individuals, and has triggered twelve wrongful detentions. Did the President anticipate these outcomes?"

"The President understood the Act would enhance security capabilities," Liam replied carefully.

"Security against what specific threats?" Torres pressed.

"I cannot discuss classified security assessments."

Senator Ramos leaned forward. "Then let's discuss public impacts. The Nashville PD used these provisions to surveil black community leaders during last week's police reform protests. The Miami-Dade Sheriff accessed private communications of four journalists investigating corruption. Is this the enhanced security you speak of?"

"Those specific cases should be reviewed for proper application—"

"But they're entirely legal under the Act your boss signed," Ramos interrupted. "Without reading it."

Walsh redirected. "Mr. Bennett, regarding resource allocation. Our preliminary review shows seventeen million dollars diverted from infrastructure improvement, veterans' services, and education programs to fund... investigations into historical matters. Can you justify these priorities?"

"National security transcends partisan budget preferences."

"Partisan?" Senator Crawford jumped in. "I authored this legislation to enhance law enforcement capabilities against real threats—terrorism, human trafficking, organized crime. Not investigations of a teenager's psychological episodes."

"The President determines threat assessment priorities," Liam stated firmly.

"Indeed she does," Crawford smiled. "Which brings us to judgment. In her first month, President Prescott has signed seventeen executive orders. Our office has confirmed she reviewed the full text of only four. Is this the meticulous leadership you've long praised?"

Liam bristled. "The presidency requires processing unprecedented volumes of information—"

"Information she apparently delegates while pursuing... alternative priorities." Crawford glanced at his notes. "Secret Service reports unusual security protocols. Unexplained evacuations of government buildings. A medical facility housing a minor without parental consent. What exactly is the President protecting us from?"

"I cannot comment on operational security measures."

"Can't or won't?" Walsh pressed. "Mr. Bennett, we're not asking for state secrets. We're asking whether the President's judgment is compromised by... unconventional beliefs."

The afternoon session brought more pointed interrogation. Senator Morrison addressed reports of million-dollar expenditures on historical document analysis. Senator Davies questioned expanded surveillance of orphanages and psychiatric facilities. Each query built toward an inevitable conclusion: the first female president was squandering her historic opportunity on paranoid fantasies.

Through it all, Liam maintained defensive lines—invoking classified status, emphasizing security priorities, protecting operational details. But exhaustion showed. By three o'clock, his carefully constructed defenses had visible cracks.

"Just one more question, Mr. Bennett," Walsh said as the afternoon wound down. "Do you believe President Prescott is mentally fit for the office she occupies?"

Before Liam could answer, Walsh continued: "The committee has one more witness today. Given the sensitive nature of these proceedings, let's proceed."

She consulted her notes. "The committee calls Senator Evelyn Harper."

The chamber's atmosphere shifted palpably. Harper entered with measured grace, her conservative gray suit projecting gravitas. She took the oath and settled herself with deliberate composure.

"Senator Harper," Walsh began, "you had occasion to meet privately with President Prescott regarding these matters?"

"I did," Harper replied. "I sought that meeting out of genuine concern for her wellbeing."

"Can you describe that meeting?"

Harper sighed softly. "The President appeared deeply troubled. She spoke about... investigations that seemed disconnected from rational security concerns. She showed me documents suggesting conspiracy theories about political opponents."

"Political opponents including yourself?"

"Yes. She seemed particularly focused on a young girl making extraordinary claims. Claims that reminded me disturbingly of my sister's descent into delusional thinking."

Walsh leaned forward. "Your sister?"

"Bella." Harper's voice caught slightly. "A brilliant woman who developed an obsession with Asher Hayes. She began seeing patterns everywhere, claiming he was still alive. Eventually, she required psychiatric care."

"And you saw similarities in the President's behavior?"

"Too many to ignore. The same fixation on impossible theories. The same dismissal of concerned advisors. The same isolation from reality." Harper paused. "I told her she needed help. She responded by initiating investigations into my personal activities."

Senator Crawford interjected: "So the President potentially weaponized federal resources against a concerned colleague?"

"I hope not intentionally," Harper replied carefully. "But her actions suggest someone not thinking clearly."

"What would you recommend?"

Harper's expression turned genuinely troubled. "With deepest respect for the office and the historic nature of her election, I believe the President needs medical evaluation. Not as punishment, but as intervention. For her own welfare and the nation's."

The committee room buzzed with reaction. Liam felt his morning's efforts crumbling as Harper's testimony provided political cover for concerns about Jordan's mental state.

Walsh called recess at four, scheduling additional proceedings for tomorrow. As cameras continued rolling, senators surrounded Harper with sympathetic words. Crawford made note of her recommendation for presidential evaluation.

Liam slipped out a side exit, phone already buzzing with urgent messages. In an empty hallway, he finally checked them:

Jordan: I watched. Evelyn's performance was masterful.

Aria: Virginia compound update. Found Bella Harper. Alive. Need immediate extraction.

Nina's medical team: Urgent. Subject experiencing rapid deterioration. Requesting presidential consultation.

He leaned against the wall, processing information that threatened to overwhelm. Harper's living sister, whose disappearance allegedly drove her to suspect possession theories? Nina's worsening condition during Jordan's public crucifixion? The Database Act transformed from mistake to weapon?

His phone rang—Jordan's direct line.

"The Bella development changes everything," she said without preamble. "If Harper's been lying about her sister's fate—"

"Jordan, they're calling for medical evaluation. Walsh wants immediate hearings. The party leadership is fracturing."

"Days. I have days." Her voice carried determination rather than fear. "Bring Aria's teams in quietly. We need Bella Harper's testimony before I'm forcibly evaluated."

"And Nina?"

"Schedule me for tonight. The facility, not video conference. I need to see what's happening myself."

After disconnecting, Liam remained in the corridor, contemplating impossible choices. Harper's credible concerns about presidential fitness. Nina's deteriorating condition. Bella Harper's sudden reappearance after months of presumed isolation.

His testimony had bought hours, not absolution. The Database Act's fallout would continue mounting. Jordan's obsession with supernatural threats would further erode credibility. And now Harper had provided the perfect narrative: a president pursuing ghosts while abandoning real governance.

As Liam drove back to the White House, twilight painted Washington in shades of amber and gray. The Capitol dome glowed with fading light while media trucks assembled outside the Justice Department—APB News preparing its evening special on Nina Foster's identity.

The woman he'd supported for decades faced elimination from office within days. Unless she could prove the impossible: that America's first female president wasn't delusional, just cursed with seeing truth others refused to acknowledge.

His phone buzzed again. A text from Senator Walsh: Private meeting tonight? Your President needs intervention, not investigation. Help us help her.

Liam stared at the message, knowing his response would determine not just Jordan's fate, but potentially the nation's. If she was right about Hayes, delaying might cost lives. If she was wrong, enabling her might cost democracy itself.

Chapter Eight

The medical wing of the secure facility hummed with state-of-the-art equipment monitoring Nina Foster's every vital sign. Jordan stood behind one-way glass, watching the girl's fitful sleep through the observation window. Dr. Elena Reeves approached with updated charts.

"The EEG patterns are extraordinary," Dr. Reeves reported quietly. "During her blackouts, her brain activity suggests multiple distinct thought processes running simultaneously—like parallel processors sharing the same hardware."

"You're saying she has multiple personalities?"

"No, Madam President. Multiple distinct consciousnesses. Her EEG shows patterns we've never documented in traditional DID cases. But here's what troubles me most—the timing is too precise. Like software with scheduled activation windows."

Jordan watched Nina's eyelids flutter. "How so?"

"The blackouts correlate exactly with significant political events. Congressional hearings. Staff meetings. Critical decisions. As if her condition is synchronized to your administration's calendar."

A knock interrupted them. Liam entered, his face ashen. "We need to talk. Now."

In the adjacent conference room, Liam spread documents across the table. "I spent the night reconstructing how the Database Act reached your desk. The bill wasn't supposed to go through normal channels—it had emergency classification that bypassed standard review."

"Who approved that classification?"

"Senator Crawford, with countersignature from..." Liam paused. "From Senator Evelyn Harper."

Jordan's mind raced. "Harper helped expedite legislation that would destroy me?"

"Or think about it differently," Liam suggested carefully. "What if she knew you'd sign it without reading? What if she wanted you to have those surveillance powers before things got worse?"

"That's insane."

"Is it? Look at this." Liam pulled up a laptop screen. "Harper's vehicle was at the Capitol the night the bill was drafted. Security footage shows her arguing with Crawford in his office. The next day, she adds protections to the bill limiting executive branch access to certain records."

Jordan studied the footage, time-stamped and officially logged. "Then why publicly attack it?"

"Cover?" Liam suggested. "If she's protecting something, she'd need plausible distance."

Before Jordan could respond, Aria burst in. "The Virginia compound. We found Bella Harper."

"Found her?" Jordan stood. "You mean her body?"

"No." Aria connected her tablet to the room's display. "Alive. In an underground medical facility with equipment that rivals ours. She's been there voluntarily, under protective protocols matching what Parker described."

"Voluntarily?"

"Says she helped design them. After recovering from Hayes's influence, she's been actively preventing others from falling into the same trap." Aria pulled up surveillance footage. "This is from yesterday."

The video showed Bella—clearly alive, clearly conscious—reviewing documents at a desk. Beside her sat another woman, conferring quietly. Jordan recognized the profile immediately.

"Is that—"

"Senator Harper," Aria confirmed. "Her sister isn't missing. She's running an operation."

Jordan's understanding realigned sharply. "Show me everything we have on Nina's placement at the orphanage."

Minutes later, a pattern emerged that chilled them all. Nina had been transferred to that specific orphanage eighteen months ago—coinciding exactly with Jordan's emergence as a presidential candidate. The transfer papers showed curious financial backing, later traced to a charitable foundation that Harper's office had occasionally supported.

"She's been watching Nina all along," Jordan realized.

"And trying to protect her," Liam added. "Look at these orphanage staff changes Harper's foundation recommended. Each replaced individual had connection to former Purist sympathizers, though never provably enough for criminal charges."

A new thought struck Jordan. "The Database Act's emergency classification was legitimate. Harper knew investigation into Nina would expose government surveillance gaps. She needed us armed before that happened."

"But couldn't appear to be helping you directly," Aria concluded. "She had to maintain political distance while secretly enabling your investigation."

Jordan returned to the observation room, studying Nina's expression. The girl was awake now, sitting up in bed with unnatural stillness. When she noticed Jordan watching, she smiled—a smile containing knowledge far beyond her fourteen years.

Through the intercom, Nina spoke: "She tried to save you too, Madam President. Just like she tried to save her sister."

"Who?"

"Senator Harper. She recognized the symptoms because she lived with them for years. Watched Bella deteriorate. Found ways to help her slowly break free." Nina's smile widened. "But you're different. The office is different. Hayes chose me specifically for you."

Jordan felt ice forming in her stomach. The calculated nature of Nina's condition—not full possession but something designed to trigger exact behaviors. A weapon calibrated to destroy presidential credibility through investigation itself.

"What are you?" she asked quietly.

"I'm exactly what I was made to be. A question you can't answer. A problem you can't solve. Every hour investigating me costs you politically. Every solution you attempt marks you as unfit. Perfect design, really."

The monitors showed Nina's vitals remaining eerily calm as she spoke these revelations. Dr. Reeves entered the observation room, reading fresh printouts.

"We're registering unusual energy signatures during her lucid periods," the doctor reported. "Not electromagnetic exactly, but something that disrupts our equipment. And look at this—" She showed brain activity charts. "The pattern suggests countdown timing. Like she's built to reach crescendo at a specific date."

"What date?"

"Two weeks from now. Coinciding with Senate impeachment proceedings if current political trajectory continues."

Jordan's phone buzzed urgently. Finn: "Madam President, we have a situation. Senator Harper is requesting immediate private meeting at the White House. Says it's about preventative measures before things escalate. She's parked outside in an unofficial vehicle, no security detail."

Through the compound facility's windows, dawn was breaking over the Virginia countryside. Jordan made rapid calculations—political suicide to meet secretly with an opponent, but possibly necessary to understand the full scale of what she faced.

"Tell her I'll meet her in the residence. Private entrance. No staff."

"And if this is a trap?" Liam asked.

"At this point, the trap has already sprung."

Thirty minutes later, Jordan faced Evelyn Harper in the Yellow Oval Room. The senator looked exhausted but focused, carrying a single briefcase.

"I know what you think of me," Harper began. "But I've been fighting this battle longer than you know."

"Your sister's alive. You've been deceiving everyone."

"Protecting everyone," Harper corrected. "Including you. Everything I've done—the investigations, the Database Act criticism, drawing media attention to your 'paranoia'—was calculated to slow your descent. Hayes's design is elegant: the more you investigate, the more you destroy yourself."

She opened the briefcase, revealing documents. "Nina's psychological profile doesn't show possession. It shows grooming. Hayes didn't take her over—he carved specific neural pathways when she was an infant. Triggered them when you were elected. She genuinely doesn't know what she contains."

Chapter Nine

The secure line buzzed at 4:47 AM. Aria Collins was already awake, reviewing surveillance reports from the Virginia compound. Ever since the initial raid, she'd maintained a skeleton crew watching the abandoned facility. Her persistence was about to pay off.

"Agent Collins?" The voice belonged to Martinez, still recovering from Montana but insisting on desk duty. "Thermal signatures just lit up Sector Three. Multiple vehicles. Heat signatures showing six—no, eight bodies entering the main building."

Aria pulled up live feeds on her encrypted tablet. There—clear as day—Victor Caine's distinctive profile moving between makeshift tables. The surveillance enhancement showed other familiar faces from Purist files: Thomas Reeves, Maria Santos, figures she'd flagged as "persons of interest" during Hayes's reign.

"Time to contact?" she asked Martinez.

"Twenty minutes ago. They've set up what looks like meeting positions. Maps on tables, documents being reviewed."

Aria's mind calculated options rapidly. By morning, Jordan would be facing Senate hearings. The Database Act fallout would dominate headlines. Meanwhile, Hayes's network was actively meeting. Evidence was slipping away as she hesitated.

She activated a secure channel to the tactical team. "Maintain positions. No approach. I'm coming to site."

Forty minutes later, Aria observed the compound through night-vision scopes. The building—officially abandoned for thirteen years—showed signs of recent renovation. Power lines had been spliced directly into underground cables. Satellite dishes pointed at strategic angles.

"We can take them," whispered Agent Hammond. "Caine and six others. We have twelve operators in position."

"Wait," Aria ordered. She pulled up thermal imaging on her tablet, studying movement patterns. "Something's off. Their positioning is too open. Like they're expecting guests."

Her secure phone buzzed. Jordan's direct line.

"Activity confirmed," Aria reported quietly. "Caine with six associates. They're reviewing documents, planning something large scale."

"Can we take them?"

"Possibly. But we need intelligence first. If we raid now, we might miss whatever they're planning."

"There has to be another way." Jordan's voice carried the strain of political pressure. The Senate hearings were tomorrow.

Aria hesitated, considering options. "There is one possibility. Parker."

"No." Jordan's response was immediate. "Absolutely not."

"Madam President, he's our only asset who could walk in there without immediate detection. Caine will recognize him, but that history might work in our favor—the prodigal returning after years in hiding."

"We'd be sending him to his death."

"We'd be gathering intelligence that could save your presidency. Maybe save the country."

Static crackled on the line as Jordan considered. Through the scope, Aria watched Caine gesture at maps on the table. Critical decisions being made while they debated ethics.

"The political reality is brutal," Jordan said finally. "The Database Act hearings tomorrow. If we have nothing concrete to show for this investigation…"

"Then it's just another conspiracy theory that destroyed your administration."

"Set it up," Jordan ordered, her voice tight. "But minimal risks. At the first sign of trouble, extraction."

The connection ended. Aria stared at her men, knowing she was about to order something that could cost lives. Military precision meant nothing against supernatural threats.

Twenty minutes later, Levi Parker stood before her, splinted fingers flexing nervously. His eyes held the same calculating intelligence she'd noticed during interrogation, but fear showed at their edges.

"You understand what we're asking," Aria said.

Parker nodded. "Thirteen years running. Now I walk back in."

"Your story is you've been in hiding. Slowly starving. Finally desperate enough to reconnect."

"And if he looks through me? Hayes could read guilt like others read newspapers. Caine learned from the master."

Aria produced a small recorder and earpiece. "Transmit everything. We'll be monitoring. First sign of trouble, we extract."

"Extract might mean cleanup after they kill me."

"That's the risk."

Parker took the equipment, securing it inside his worn jacket. "If I have to die stopping this, at least it's for something."

He approached the compound alone. Through thermal imaging, Aria watched him pause at the door—a moment's hesitation—before entering. The guards let him pass without searching. First mistake.

The listening devices activated immediately. Parker's voice, careful and measured: "Victor. Been a long time."

Caine's response was warm. "Levi. Heard you'd gone completely underground."

"Had to. After Montana. After what happened."

"Come in. We're planning. Hayes would want you here."

Aria adjusted frequencies, catching every word. Parker moved deeper into the building. The team tracked his position through thermal gradients.

"The girl's in place," Caine continued. "Everything's moving according to design. Just need final confirmation on the trigger."

"What trigger?"

A pause stretched infinitely. Then Caine's voice changed—colder, more analytical. "Strange phrase. Someone truly out of touch would ask 'trigger for what?' You asked 'what trigger?' Like someone who already knows the plan."

"Victor, I don't follow—"

"Your walk, Levi. The way you hold your damaged hand. Not like someone who broke it climbing mountains." Caine's footsteps circled in the audio feed. "More like someone recently... interrogated."

Panic flashed across Parker's thermal signature. "I took precautions—"

"Of course you did. Same precautions you'd take if federal agents prepared you for this exact situation."

The gunshot was impossibly loud through the speakers. Parker's thermal image flared, then collapsed. Aria's hand gripped her radio, preparing to order assault.

"Stand down," Caine's voice commanded. "The watchers in the trees. We know you're there. Take Parker. Consider him our message."

Aria activated her comm. "All teams, weapons down. They've made us."

Through the scopes, they watched Caine's group exit the building methodically. Six figures moving with trained precision toward vehicles parked behind the facility. No rush. No concern.

"Should we follow?" Hammond asked tensely.

"No. They've given us Parker. Let's see why."

The tactical team waited twenty minutes before advancing. Aria led the entry, weapon raised but unnecessary. Parker lay in the central room, a single shot to the chest. Blood pooled beneath him, stark against grey concrete.

"Multiple exit wounds," their medic reported. "Close range, high caliber. Professional execution."

Aria knelt beside the body. Parker's eyes stared at nothing, but his left hand clutched something—a small cloth bundle pressed against his jacket. She extracted it carefully.

Inside lay a leather journal, pristine despite the blood. The first page bore a single sentence in precise handwriting:

Hayes died as reported. But his legacy was engineered to transcend death.

She read quickly, translating aloud for her team:

"Nina Foster wasn't possessed—she was programmed. Hayes spent months as an infant creating neural pathways, planting specific response patterns. Upon hearing election news of the first female president, these pathways activated. She was driven to seek out Secret Service contact. A mole within the department was briefed to take her claim seriously."

Aria flipped pages. "The entire investigation is a triggered response. Every piece of evidence we find confirms Hayes is alive, while destroying the president's credibility. Perfect political poison."

"But if Hayes is dead..." Hammond began.

"Then we're fighting ghosts he created fourteen years ago. Programming so precise it predicts and responds to events he couldn't have known would happen."

The journal continued detailing the mechanism: how infant trauma creates malleable consciousness, how specific trigger phrases activate pre-programmed responses, how the investigation itself feeds the psychological pattern.

"Call President Prescott," Aria ordered. "We need quarantine protocols on Nina. This isn't possession—it's the most sophisticated sleeper agent program in history."

As her team secured the compound, Aria reviewed remaining pages. Names appeared: government officials who knew about the program. Safe houses where inactive subjects waited. Protocols for cleaning up the inevitable mess.

The final entry stopped her:

May 15, 2000 - Final Project Note

If executed correctly, the first female president will destroy herself chasing my ghost. The beauty of programming versus possession: the subject genuinely believes. No torture can extract what isn't deliberately hidden. No medication can treat what isn't illness. And when truth emerges, it arrives too late to save anything.

Victory through victim's own hand. The perfect assassination.

Aria closed the journal, its weight somehow heavier than leather and paper should allow. Outside, dawn painted the Virginia hills in shades of amber and gray. They'd found their truth, but at what cost? Parker's sacrifice had revealed the enemy was far more insidious than supernatural possession— it was psychological engineering so advanced it mimicked the impossible.

She initiated secure upload protocols, transmitting everything to Jordan. The investigation had taken another impossible turn. Hayes wasn't haunting them from beyond death. He'd planted time bombs in human minds years before his execution.

As extraction teams processed the scene, Aria considered implications spreading like contamination. If Nina was programmed, how many others waited for election triggers? How many government officials carried dormant directives?

The conspiracy wasn't supernatural—it was terrifyingly scientific. And they were racing against programming that adapted to counter every investigative move.

Her phone buzzed. Jordan: "Received package. Initiating new protocols. Nice work."

But was it? They'd solved one mystery only to uncover another. Hayes had won by making them chase possession while real programming executed perfectly.

Parker's body waited for extraction, positioned deliberately where they'd find it. Even in death, Caine had sent a message: We know what you're doing. We're five steps ahead.

Aria sealed the compound, knowing they'd likely never return. The real battleground had shifted to the White House, where a programmed teenager held the presidency hostage without even realizing her role.

The drive back to Washington felt longer than it had any right to. The journal rested in Aria's briefcase, evidence that might save Jordan politically while destroying hope of simple solutions. They weren't fighting ghosts. They were fighting the most advanced psychological warfare ever deployed against American democracy.

As her vehicle crossed into Maryland, Aria's phone rang. Dr. Reeves: "Activity at the medical facility. Nina Foster just triggered an unexpected response to her medication protocol. Her vital signs showed impossible readings before returning to normal."

"Elaborate."

"For seventeen seconds, her heart rate flatlined. No pulse. Brain activity went completely blank. Then sudden return to normal function. The monitors recorded seven distinct neural patterns during that period - far beyond any multiple personality disorder presentation."

Aria gripped the steering wheel tighter. They weren't dealing with possession. They were dealing with programming so sophisticated it could temporarily shut down biological functions and create artificial personalities on demand.

Hayes had truly died thirteen years ago. But his ghost was already inside the White House, wearing the skin of a traumatized teenager, executing the perfect political assassination.

Chapter Ten

The Situation Room felt smaller with its five occupants, the walls seeming to press inward as Jordan spread Parker's journal across the conference table. The photographs taken at the Virginia compound flanked it—shrine to possession, maps of power structures, the mirror inscribed with her inauguration date.

"We need to discuss what this means." Jordan's voice carried the steady authority that had served her as prosecutor and president, though exhaustion shadowed her features. She'd read the journal three times during the night, memorizing entries that threatened to reshape everything they'd pursued.

Aria cleared her throat, opening her encrypted tablet. "I'll summarize the key revelations: Asher Hayes died in February 2000 as reported. The footage wasn't doctored. The cremation happened. He's dead."

A collective exhale moved through the room—the sound of thirteen years of questions finding imperfect answers.

"But," Aria continued, "before his death, Hayes developed a program to engineer specific psychological responses in child subjects. Nina Foster was abducted specifically for this purpose. During the time he held her—less than twenty-four hours—he implemented what he called 'neural pathway architecture.'"

Liam leaned forward. "Programming a one-year-old in twenty-four hours? How?"

"The journal doesn't provide specifics on methodology," Aria admitted. "Only results. Upon hearing news of the first female president's election, specific triggers activated in Nina's brain. She was compelled to seek out presidential contact. A mole within Secret Service was briefed to take her claims seriously."

Theo Marshall's pen tapped steadily against his notepad. "So our entire investigation was choreographed by dead man's contingency plan?"

"According to this." Jordan touched the leather binding. "Hayes predicted the eventual election of a female president. Created multiple assets to activate upon that news. Nina was his primary weapon—designed to generate an investigation that would consume resources and credibility."

Finn Sullivan reviewed his own notes, tablet screen reflecting off his glasses. "The investigation itself was the trap. Every hour studying allegedly supernatural threats decreased your approval rating. Every dollar spent searching for Asher Hayes painted you as obsessed, paranoid."

"The Database Act signing," Liam interjected bitterly. "Perfect manipulation. You were so distracted by Nina's testimony that you signed legislation without proper review. He even accounted for your tendency to focus intensely on priority cases."

Jordan felt cold settling in her stomach. "The journal contains detailed psychological profiles on all of us. How we think. How we react to stress. Our decision patterns."

Aria pulled up digital scans on the wall display. "There's more. Names of other 'assets'—children programmed like Nina. Locations of Purist safe houses. Communication networks that remained active long after Hayes's death. It's a complete intelligence package."

Silence stretched as the implications accumulated. Outside the Situation Room, morning sunlight painted the West Wing in stark geometric patterns.

"This is almost too clean," Liam said finally. "Everything we need to understand the threat. Complete operational details. Even the names of his network still operating today."

"Exactly what I was thinking," Theo agreed. "Hayes develops psychological weapons for over a year, programs multiple children, creates vast networks—and details everything conveniently in a journal delivered by his second-in-command?"

Aria set down her tablet slowly. "I've interrogated dozens of operatives over my career. Caine's behavior was completely contrary to type. Former Purists protect information above all else. They die before talking. Caine executed Parker to maintain operational security, then left us a complete blueprint?"

"The timing," Finn observed, checking his watch. "Tomorrow's Senate hearings on the Database Act. APB News leaked story about investigating Evelyn Harper. Congress demanding explanations. And suddenly we receive definitive answers that make the supernatural angle disappear?"

Jordan moved to the window, watching staff cross the South Lawn. Impossible decisions crystallized around her. "We're being given exactly what we need to explain away thirteen years of investigation. A rational answer to irrational questions."

"But," Aria began carefully, "it doesn't explain Nina's seventeen-second flatline. Or the seven distinct neural patterns. Or her accurate knowledge of classified Purist operations."

"The quantum physics," Liam added. "A fourteen-year-old displaying graduate-level understanding during programmed states?"

Theo's pen continued its steady rhythm. "What if the journal is strategic misdirection? Lead us toward psychological explanations when the truth is still possession?"

"Or," Finn suggested, "what if it's both? Programming that created vulnerability to supernatural influence?"

Jordan turned back to the table, political reality warring with implications that defied comprehension. The Database Act hearings tomorrow would demand explanations. Her approval ratings continued their precipitous decline. Every day investigating strengthened calls for her medical evaluation.

"We need verification," she decided. "Aria, discretely monitor the safe houses listed. Confirm if Caine's group actually uses them. If this journal is disinformation, physical surveillance might reveal truth."

"And Nina?" Aria asked.

"Continues medical observation. Dr. Reeves will dig deeper into the seventeen-second incident. I want to understand if programming alone explains everything we've witnessed."

"Madam President," Finn interjected carefully, "we should prepare communication strategy. If the journal's legitimate, it gives us explanation for investigation costs. If it's disinformation, we need defense against whatever's coming."

"Draft two scenarios," Jordan ordered. "One acknowledging Hayes's posthumous program as legitimate national security threat. One maintaining investigation due to ongoing concerns despite received information."

Theo clicked his pen closed. "And if tomorrow's hearings push for conclusive evidence? If Senator Harper produces her sister's research suggesting the journal confirms their mental illness theory?"

The question hung heavy in the morning air. Jordan reviewed accumulated choices—each path forward carrying enormous risk. Accepting the journal as truth might appease political pressure while potentially missing deeper threats. Dismissing it might prove correct but accelerate her presidency's destruction.

"We continue balanced approach," she stated finally. "Investigate the journal's claims while maintaining protocols for supernatural possibilities. But carefully—very carefully."

As the meeting adjourned, each participant carried different weights. Aria questioned thirteen years hunting a dead man. Liam wondered if his friend remained trapped in delusion. Theo calculated political mathematics that grew more complex hourly. Finn prepared narratives designed to satisfy demands for explanation without confirming impossible realities.

Jordan remained alone in the Situation Room, Parker's journal before her. Its leather binding bore no supernatural energy, no indication of the remarkable claims within. Yet that normalcy felt deceptive—just another layer in Hayes's meticulously designed deception.

Her secure phone buzzed. Message from Aria: "First surveillance team reports two listed safe houses abandoned for years. Third shows recent activity—but it's squatters, not Purist operations. Beginning to suspect strategic misdirection."

Jordan typed back: "Continue verification. Document everything. Prepare for possibility journal deliberately leads us away from real threats."

Jordan stepped into the Oval Office, mind still processing the cabinet meeting's revelations. The morning's events had reshaped their understanding of the threat—Hayes dead but his weapons still active, precision-engineered rather than supernatural.

Evelyn Harper rose from one of the wingback chairs. The senator who normally exuded polished authority now looked haggard, dark circles shadowing her eyes. In her trembling hands, she clutched a phone displaying a single text message.

"We need to talk. Immediately."

Jordan felt fatigue pressing against her shoulders. "Senator Harper, we've established protocols for—"

"Bella's missing."

The words dropped like stones into still water. Jordan moved behind her desk, buying time to process this new crisis.

"Your sister? The one you warned me about—"

"Don't." Evelyn's composure cracked slightly. "I knew you'd found her at the compound. Aria's surveillance team spotted her weeks ago. When I warned you about mental illness, I was counting on whoever might be monitoring our conversation to believe I was dismissing her research as delusion."

Jordan studied Evelyn carefully. "You were protecting her through misdirection."

"Her safety depended on everyone believing she was incompetent. Even you couldn't officially acknowledge her presence without exposing her to Hayes's network."

"Explain."

"She was at the compound. Virginia. Protected wing, underground level—my arrangement. After the initial investigation found her, I authorized enhanced security protocols." Evelyn's control cracked, voice shaking. "Your team raided last night. In the chaos with Parker, checking the journal's claims—did anyone verify her location?"

Jordan reached for her secure phone, already knowing the answer. "Aria?"

Within moments, the National Security Advisor appeared on video feed from the Situation Room. Her exhaustion matched everyone else's.

"Status on secondary subjects at Virginia compound?" Jordan asked tersely.

Aria's expression shifted from professional to concerned to alarmed. "Secondary subjects? We focused on primary objectives—Parker, the journal, immediate intelligence gathering. The medical wing... we didn't..." She turned off screen, barking commands. "Team reports?"

Through the connection, Jordan heard frantic keyboard typing, radio chatter.

"Madam President," Aria returned. "Level B medical facility showed signs of recent abandonment. We have thermal signatures from three days ago but assumed squatters or maintenance. We never verified specific identity of occupants."

Evelyn sank into the chair. "Bella wasn't supposed to leave those rooms. The protocols, the safety measures—she understood the risks."

"When did you last have contact?" Jordan demanded.

"Two days ago. She called about the increased activity she'd noticed. Caine's group moving between buildings. She seemed frightened, said their patterns were different this time." Evelyn's finger found a picture on her phone. "This came an hour ago."

The image showed Bella Harper seated at a desk, clearly photographed in low light. Behind her stood two figures—shadows with vaguely human shapes. Text below the image read: She helped us understand. Now she helps us implement.

"Helped you understand what?" Jordan asked the absent photographers.

"The programming," Evelyn whispered. "Bella spent years reverse-engineering Hayes's methods. She developed countermeasures, ways to break the conditioning. If they have her..." She left the implications unspoken.

Jordan leaned back, calculating rapidly. The journal offered neat explanations while this abduction suggested ongoing operations. "Was she involved in the medical evaluation of Nina?"

"Consulting remotely. The patterns were so similar to her own experience."

Aria's voice came through the secure line: "Team confirms full evacuation of medical wing. They found equipment for EEG manipulation, psychological pattern recording, cognitive behavior modification tech. Nothing taken, just abandoned."

"Or they have everything they need," Evelyn countered. "Bella's research filled the gaps in Hayes's original programming. She was trying to help children like Nina break free. If Caine's group has that knowledge…"

Jordan stood, political crisis expanding exponentially. "They can either deprogram Hayes's victims—"

"Or create better ones," Aria finished grimly. "Madam President, if hostile assets have Dr. Harper's research, our ability to counteract the programming becomes their ability to enhance it."

"We raid them," Jordan stated. "Track the message source, mobilize—"

"The photo came through five proxy servers across three countries," Evelyn interrupted. "Bella established those routes for her protection. They're using her own security measures against us."

Through the windows, afternoon sun painted the Rose Garden in stark relief. Jordan contemplated cascading failures—the journal providing answers that distracted from disappearances, investigations that left critical subjects unmonitored, the endless chess game where each piece captured revealed two more in play.

"Options?" she asked her core team.

"The safe houses Parker's journal lists," Aria suggested. "We accelerate surveillance. If they took Bella for her research, they need somewhere to implement it."

"Increased monitoring of all Nina-like cases," Evelyn added. "Bella maintained files on sixteen children showing similar patterns. If they start activating them—"

"We'd have coordinated assets triggering across the country," Jordan completed.

Her intercom buzzed. Finn's voice carried unusual strain: "Madam President? I need you to see this. Now."

On the wall display, CNN showed breaking coverage: "Hospital in Denver reports seven children admitted with identical symptoms: sudden onset seizures, speaking in languages they don't know, displaying impossible knowledge. Ages 12-15, all adopted."

The anchor continued: "Medical staff describes it as 'simultaneous psychological breaks.' Authorities haven't determined the cause, but Senator Crawford calls it 'evidence of dangerous experimental psychological programs.'"

Evelyn gripped the armrest. "It's starting."

"Or they're testing," Aria countered. "Bella's disappearance, the Denver cases—coordinated demonstration of capability?"

Jordan's political calculations accelerated. Tomorrow's hearings now faced dual crises—the Database Act investigation and potential evidence of mass child psychological warfare.

"Aria, split teams. Alpha continues Denver investigation. Bravo tracks Bella's potential locations. Charlie maintains Nina protocols. We can't chase everything, but we can't ignore anything."

"Budget concerns?" Liam had entered quietly, holding congressional correspondence. "Senator Walsh just delivered formal request for full accounting of investigation costs. They'll demand justification for expanded operations."

"Then they'll get it," Jordan decided. "Draft emergency executive briefing. If Hayes's psychological weapons are activating nationwide, we have mandate for full response."

The afternoon dissolved into crisis management. Aria coordinated multi-state surveillance. Liam drafted political containment strategies. Finn prepared for media avalanche when Denver story expanded.

But through the chaos, Jordan's mind kept returning to Evelyn's haunted expression as she described her sister. The senator who'd spent months opposing, undermining, criticizing—all while secretly trying to save others from Bella's fate. Now that protection had crumbled, and the enemy held keys to Hayes's most sophisticated weapon.

As evening approached, Aria returned with updates: "Denver cases all trace to same adoption agency. Closed twelve years ago after founder's death. Records destroyed in 'routine audit mistake.' But we found connection—agency CEO was Marie Driscoll, former Purist logistics coordinator. She disappeared months before Hayes's death. Everyone assumed she'd been killed by Hayes to tie up loose ends."

"Assumed wrong." Jordan reviewed patient reports scrolling past. "Twelve years managing an adoption agency, placing children in specific homes, then vanishing with Hayes?" Seven children, diverse backgrounds, adopted between ages two and five—prime programming window according to Bella's research. "Activation timing?"

"Synchronized with Parker's death. Like they needed both the journal as misdirection and Bella's capture as escalation trigger."

"Permission to initiate rapid response protocols?" Aria asked. "If the Denver cases represent first wave, we need countermeasures before tomorrow morning."

Jordan weighed authorization that stretched executive power beyond comfortable boundaries. Medical intervention without parental consent. Interstate law enforcement coordination without state approval. Resource deployment at unprecedented scale.

Yet the alternative—waiting for congressional approval while programmed children seized across the nation—seemed exponentially worse.

"Granted. But document everything. We'll face judgment later. Right now we prevent catastrophe."

As Aria departed to implement emergency protocols, Jordan found herself alone with Evelyn. The senator who'd staged public opposition while privately enabling Jordan's investigation now sat vulnerable in enemy crossfire.

"They took her to hurt you through me," Evelyn said quietly. "Hayes's programming even accounted for political alliances he couldn't have predicted."

"Or," Jordan suggested carefully, "Bella left willingly. Found something in his design so elegant she couldn't resist completing it."

Evelyn's sharp intake of breath signaled hit striking home. Jordan had prosecuted enough cases to recognize when truth's possibility shattered composure.

"No. Bella would never—"

"Then help me find her," Jordan interrupted. "Your resources, your knowledge of her methods, your political cover—we need all of it. Tonight's actions determine tomorrow's world."

Through the evening, as Washington prepared for imminent hearings that would likely erupt into constitutional crisis, Jordan orchestrated operations that either validated her presidency or confirmed her enemies' warnings: America's first female president losing grip on reality while chasing ghosts only she believed existed.

But the ghosts were children. And their seizures were real.

Chapter Eleven

The Oval Office door opened quietly. Jordan didn't look up from the stack of documents in front of her—third-quarter education budgets that seemed meaningless given the crisis unfolding across the country.

"Good evening, Madam President."

She glanced up sharply. Michael stood in the doorway holding two takeout bags, wearing his deliberately formal expression.

"Michael?" She checked her watch. Nearly nine o'clock. "What are you—"

"Your husband thought you might need dinner." He set the bags on the coffee table. "Though I understand I'm supposed to address you as 'Madam President' during business hours."

Jordan felt a smile tug at her lips—the first in days. "That's only for state occasions."

"Ah. Then I'll try again." He moved to her desk, took both her hands, and kissed her properly. "Hi, sweetheart. You're working too late."

"I'm always working too late."

"Not like this." He nudged her toward the couch. "When was our last real conversation? Not counting you falling asleep mid-sentence."

"Michael, there's so much happening—"

"Which is why you need twenty minutes to eat actual food instead of whatever Liam leaves in your inbox."

She allowed herself to be led to the couch, papers still clutched in one hand. Michael unpacked Thai food—her favorite from the place near their old apartment. The normalcy felt alien, like wearing an unfamiliar costume.

"How's the new semester?" she asked, scanning a budget revision while speaking.

"Someone's not listening."

"I am. Tenure committee approved your new course on executive power limitations. Very timely." She signed off on the revision without reading the footnotes.

"Jordan." Michael gently took the papers. "I realize being president is demanding, but this isn't just longer hours. You're somewhere else entirely."

"I told you this would be difficult."

"Difficult, yes. Transformative, no." He studied her face. "You used to know everything I was working on. Now I mention a course you approved personally, and you clearly have no idea what I'm talking about."

She opened her mouth to argue, but her phone buzzed. Aria's name flashed on the screen.

"I need to—"

"Of course you do." Michael stood abruptly. "God forbid anything interrupt the all-consuming investigation."

"Michael—"

"What is it, Jordan? Really? Because the woman I married would never sign legislation without reading it. Would never investigate a senator based on a teenager's word. Would never—"

Her phone buzzed again. Two urgent messages from Liam.

"I'm sorry. I truly am. But I need to take this." She lifted the phone. "It could be important."

"More important than us?" But he was already collecting his coat. "Enjoy your dinner, Madam President."

The Oval Office door closed behind him with careful softness, somehow worse than if he'd slammed it. Jordan stared at the Thai food cooling on the table, pad thai growing cold and forgotten as another piece of her old life slipped quietly away.

Her phone buzzed insistently. Two urgent messages from Liam.

"Madam President - Walsh just added surprise witness to tomorrow's roster. No name given."

"Need to discuss immediately. Coming over."

Jordan set down her phone, dread settling like ice in her stomach. Walsh wouldn't add a witness this late unless it was explosive. She looked at the pad thai congealing in its container—Michael's attempt at normalcy already ruined by whatever crisis approached.

Three minutes later, Liam entered without his usual knock. His face was ashen, dark circles beneath bloodshot eyes. He'd clearly been up all night monitoring the political situation.

"Who's the witness?" Jordan asked immediately.

"Jasper Reed."

The words hit her like a physical blow. Jordan sank back against the couch cushions. "Jasper? But he's been on our side. He brought us Nina. He helped us—"

"Helped us start the investigation that's destroying your presidency," Liam finished quietly. He moved to the window, staring out at the darkened South Lawn. "Think about it, Jordan. He had Nina ready immediately. Day one of your administration. That level of access?"

"You think he's been...?" Jordan couldn't finish the thought.

"Possessed? Programmed? Something." Liam turned back to face her. "His memory gaps about the file destruction. The way he seemed to know just enough about Hayes to be helpful but not suspicious. He orchestrated bringing Nina to you perfectly."

Jordan's prosecutorial mind began connecting patterns with growing horror. "He kept referring her back to us. Pushing the investigation forward whenever we considered pulling back."

"And now he's going to testify against you tomorrow," Liam continued. "Whatever he says will carry enormous weight. Former president, respected elder statesman. The Senate will hang on his every word."

Jordan stood, pacing behind her desk. "If Hayes got to Jasper..."

"Then we've been played from day one. He had a man inside before you ever took the oath."

"That inaugural meeting. How did Jasper even get Nina to us so quickly? The logistics alone..."

"Unless he planned it. Unless he was waiting for this moment—for you to take office."

Jordan felt her carefully constructed investigation collapsing. Every decision she'd made, every resource allocated, every political capital spent—all potentially guided by Hayes's possessed puppet.

"Can we prove possession?" she asked.

"How? We can't exactly march Jasper to Aria's medical team for brain scans hours before he testifies." Liam slumped into a chair. "The political reality is brutal. Tomorrow morning, a beloved former president will testify against you. No proof of possession will save you from that."

"What if he reveals something during testimony? Shows signs?"

"Who would believe it? More paranoid delusions from President Prescott. Seeing possession everywhere she looks."

Jordan stared at her reflection in the darkened window. The woman who'd sworn to preserve, protect, and defend now faced an enemy who'd infiltrated the highest office before her election was even announced.

"Call Aria," she decided. "We need protocols for tomorrow. If Jasper is compromised, we watch for signs. Facial cues. Voice modulation. Anything that might suggest—"

Her phone buzzed again. A news alert: "Ex-President Reed Files Supplemental Testimony: Cites 'Recently Recovered Memories' About Transition Period Concerns."

Liam's expression grew even grimmer. "They're getting ahead of any possession theory. 'Recovered memories' sounds medical. Professional. Not supernatural."

"Then we document everything tonight." Jordan's voice carried the determination that had built her prosecutorial career. "Every interaction with Jasper. Every decision he influenced. If we're going down tomorrow, we're taking the truth with us."

As Liam moved to the secure phone, Jordan remained at the window. Across Washington, normal lives continued while her world narrowed to a single question: how deep did Hayes's influence extend within her own administration?

The pad thai sat abandoned on the coffee table. Michael's disappointed departure felt like a different lifetime, already overshadowed by tomorrow's existential threat. Even in this dark moment, Jordan couldn't help but wonder if Michael intended to leave her too. Just like everyone else had.

Liam was still staring at her, waiting for direction, when Jordan's prosecutorial mind clicked into place. Twenty years of building cases based on evidence that could be verified. But what if verification required witnessing the impossible?

"Call an emergency meeting," she said, already moving toward her secure phone. "Aria, Theo, and Dr. Reeves. Now."

"Jordan, what are you—"

"Tomorrow isn't the end. It's the beginning." She punched in Aria's number. "And I need Jasper Reed to be the one who proves it."

Thirty minutes later, they gathered in the West Wing Situation Room. Jordan spread documents across the table—Senate procedural rules, building schematics, medical reports on possession triggers.

"Jasper testifies tomorrow morning. He's possessed. We're going to prove it in front of the entire Senate."

Aria studied the room layout. "Security protocols?"

"Minimal. We can't prevent it, but we control our own people." Jordan turned to Dr. Reeves. "Nina's condition. Can she demonstrate controlled possession on command?"

"Theoretically. The trigger phrases are documented. But the medical risks—"

"Outweigh national security?" Jordan leaned forward. "I need one clean demonstration. A few minutes, maximum. Can you prepare her?"

Dr. Reeves nodded reluctantly. "We'd need intensive preparation overnight. And contingency protocols if—"

"Theo," Jordan interrupted. "You'll take Nina's medical team. If I give the extraction code, you evacuate her immediately."

The Vice President absorbed this, his usual charm replaced by grim understanding. "You realize if this fails, we've committed to confirming every conspiracy theory about government mind control experiments?"

"And if we do nothing?" She gestured at the timeline. "By noon tomorrow, constitutional crisis begins. By week's end, Hayes's network activates every programmed asset. This is our window."

Liam finally spoke. "The Senate won't just let you interrupt—"

"Article 1, Section 5—the President may address grievances directly to a Senate investigatory committee." Jordan's voice carried the confidence of her prosecutor days. "Especially when national security is at stake. Walsh can argue, but she can't stop me."

"And Nina's willing to do this?"

Jordan picked up a transcript of their latest conversation. "She asked me yesterday what happens if no one believes. I told her I'd find a way to make them believe."

The room fell silent as the implications settled. They weren't just preventing political assassination. They were forcing reality itself to bend before the Senate.

"Aria," Jordan continued, "I need your team positioned for multiple outcomes. If Jasper's possession manifests violently—"

"Already mapping tactical positions. But if he tries to leave—"

"He won't. That's the beauty of Hayes's design. He can't run without confirming everything I've claimed. His own trap forces him to stay."

Two hours later, as her staff executed preparations, Jordan called Michael. He answered on the fourth ring, voice thick with sleep.

"They're calling for my medical evaluation," she said without preamble. "Tomorrow they'll likely vote to remove me from office."

"Jordan—"

"I wanted you to know that whatever happens tomorrow, I'm not crazy. I'm just the first to see what's coming."

The line went quiet. Then: "I know."

She ended the call, returning to the medical wing where Nina waited, IVs and monitors tracking her vitals. The girl looked up as Jordan entered.

"Tomorrow," Nina said, "I show them what you've known all along."

"Are you sure?"

Nina managed a smile too knowing for fourteen years. "They need to see what hides beneath the surface. Besides," her voice dropped, "he wants me to stay quiet. That's how I know we're doing the right thing."

Chapter Twelve

The medical facility hummed with pre-dawn activity as Jordan stood outside Nina's room, reviewing her notes one final time. She'd prosecuted trials with less at stake, though none where the defendant's guilt or innocence could reshape reality itself.

"EEG indicates stable baseline," Dr. Reeves reported, adjusting monitors that tracked Nina's brain activity. "The trigger phrases we've isolated should produce controlled manifestation. Thirty seconds minimum, five minutes maximum before risk of neural damage."

"And if it exceeds five minutes?" Jordan asked, her prosecutor's mind demanding contingencies.

"We use the emergency sedative protocol." Dr. Reeves glanced at preparation trays. "But that might itself be incriminating. Heavily sedating a minor during congressional testimony..."

"Won't matter if we fail." Aria checked her watch. "Team positions confirmed. Theo's at the medical fallback point. Chen and Hammond stationed for extraction if needed."

Through the observation window, Jordan watched Nina meditate with impossible stillness for a fourteen-year-old. The girl's training over the past forty-eight hours had been intensive—learning to surrender control without losing herself completely. Hayes's programming demanded precision.

Dr. Reeves handed Jordan a small device. "Biometric monitor. If Nina's heart rate crosses two hundred or drops below forty, press the red button. It triggers immediate intervention."

"And tips our hand," Jordan noted, pocketing the device. "We get one shot at this. One controlled demonstration of what Hayes created."

"Madam President." Aria's voice carried unusual gravity. "I've been thinking about Jasper. If he is possessed, and we force manifestation…"

"He'll either expose himself or accelerate whatever endgame Hayes planned." Jordan's expression remained steady. "Either outcome serves truth."

Liam burst through the doors, face flushed with urgency. "Walsh moved up the hearing by two hours. Jasper's already at the Capitol. They're painting this as a final intervention before you're declared unfit."

"Perfect." Jordan strode toward Nina's room. "Then we match their urgency with revelation."

Inside, Nina opened her eyes at Jordan's entrance. Dark circles couldn't hide the unnatural awareness behind her gaze—knowledge no child should possess battling with genuine youth.

"He knows," Nina said quietly. "Hayes. He's been watching through me these past days. He believes we'll fail because you care too much about procedure. About evidence. About playing by rules he abandoned long ago."

"Then he hasn't learned who I am," Jordan replied. "I built my career on cases everyone said were unwinnable. Juries that believed impossible stories if you present them correctly."

"This isn't a jury of your peers."

"No." Jordan knelt to meet Nina's eyes. "It's harder. It's people desperate to believe their reality is safe. Are you ready to show them it isn't?"

Nina nodded, standing with mechanical precision. "The first phrase triggers memory recall. The second opens access to Hayes's imprinted knowledge. The third…"

"The third activates full integration." Jordan gripped the girl's shoulders. "But you maintain core self. His knowledge, not his control. Can you hold that distinction?"

"For the time we need, yes."

Twenty minutes later, Jordan's motorcade sliced through Washington's early morning traffic. In the back of the armored Suburban, Nina sat between Aria and Agent Chen, an earpiece allowing Dr. Reeves to monitor her condition remotely.

"Remember," Jordan counseled, "we're not performing for sympathy. We're demonstrating irrefutable evidence of a national security threat. No drama. Clinical precision."

Nina's laugh held Hayes's distinctive cadences—practice bleeding through. "You sound like my professor who never existed. Which is how I know I'm ready."

The girl's comment sent ice through Jordan's veins. If Hayes was monitoring through Nina, he knew every detail of their plan. But knowing and preventing were different matters. His own design trapped him— possession required proximity, engagement, interaction. To stop them, he'd have to expose himself.

"Remember the extraction signals," Aria reviewed quietly. "Green light in my earpiece, continue demonstration. Yellow, thirty-second warning. Red, immediate evacuation."

Jordan studied Washington's familiar monuments sliding past the windows. As a prosecutor, she'd approached the steps of the Supreme Court dozens of times. But never to force an entire government to face truth it desperately wished to deny.

"Madam President?" The driver's voice interrupted her thoughts. "Protesters at the Capitol. Several hundred. Signs calling for resignation."

"Of course." Jordan adjusted her suit jacket. "No presidency crumbles quietly."

Liam consulted his phone. "APB News running real-time coverage. Their headline: 'President's Last Stand.' They're positioning this as your final desperate action before inevitable removal."

"Then they're paying attention." Jordan checked her own device. "Perfect viewership for our demonstration."

The Suburban rounded the final corner, and the Capitol Building materialized through morning haze. Television trucks lined the plaza, satellite dishes aimed like accusatory fingers. Protesters pressed against barriers, their signs alternating between supportive pleas and calls for medical evaluation.

"Medical evaluation," Jordan murmured, a smile touching her lips. "How perfectly ironic."

Secret Service agents surrounded their vehicle, executing precise extraction protocols. Through tinted windows, Jordan glimpsed Jasper Reed's approach—his bearing still commanding despite seventy-three years, moving with purpose toward the building that had defined his life.

"Remember," she told Nina one final time, "Hayes may know we're coming, but his arrogance is his weakness. He believes his design is perfect. That no one would dare force truth into daylight."

"Unlike you," Nina observed, "who spent twenty years dragging truth into every courtroom in America."

Jordan exited the vehicle into camera flashes and shouted questions. She moved with deliberate confidence toward the Capitol steps, ignoring reporters' calls about her "impending psychiatric evaluation." Secret Service agents flanked her, Nina invisible within their protective formation.

Inside the rotunda, the familiar acoustics carried echoed

conversation from the Senate chamber. Jordan paused, gathering herself for what would either save or destroy everything she'd built.

"Time?" she asked Liam.

"Eight-thirteen. Walsh has already gaveled the session open. Jasper's being sworn in now."

"Then we're precisely where we need to be." Jordan adjusted her lapel pin—the silver key presented at inauguration. "Let's give the Senate its demonstration."

They entered through the back gallery, positioning themselves strategically near the exit. From their vantage point, Jordan observed the chamber filling with senators, media representatives, and senior staff. Walsh presided from her elevated position, her expression carrying the gravity of someone orchestrating history.

Jasper Reed took the witness stand with dignified bearing. From a distance, nothing suggested extraordinary about America's forty-sixth president. But Jordan watched for telltale signs—the slight hesitation between thoughts, the practiced expressions that didn't quite match emotional context.

"Mr. President," Walsh began formally, "thank you for providing this chamber with additional clarity on matters of national importance."

"Of course, Senator. The peaceful transfer of power requires honest assessment." Jasper's voice carried its familiar authority. "Though it pains me to speak of a successor's... instability."

Jordan felt Nina shift beside her. The girl's breathing had changed—something Hayes recognized in Jasper triggering response in his other vessel.

"Please proceed with your statement," Walsh encouraged.

"During the transition period, I observed concerning behaviors," Jasper began, consulting notes with mechanical precision. "President Prescott exhibited fixation on unsubstantiated security threats. She repeatedly requested files on individuals long deceased. Her questions suggested preoccupation with conspiracy theories rather than governance priorities."

The senators leaned forward collectively, absorbing testimony that painted Jordan as unfit from her first days in office. Walsh nodded approvingly as Jasper detailed specific incidents that seemed damning in isolation.

"Most troubling was her immediate credibility given to a disturbed minor's claims," Jasper continued. "Without proper verification protocols, she diverted millions in resources to investigate fantasies."

Jordan's hand found the emergency alert in her pocket, fingers tracing the device's smooth surface. Not yet. Let him build the case that would become his own destruction.

"In your professional opinion," Walsh pressed, "did these behaviors indicate compromised judgment unsuitable for presidential authority?"

"Reluctantly, yes." Jasper's expression conveyed appropriate gravity. "The office demands absolute mental clarity. When reality becomes negotiable, leadership becomes impossible."

"When reality becomes negotiable." Walsh emphasized the phrase. "A troubling assessment from someone who knows the presidency's demands intimately."

"For the nation's sake," Jasper concluded, "I recommend immediate evaluation under the Twenty-Fifth Amendment. President Prescott requires medical assistance, not impeachment."

The chamber buzzed with the weight of a former president declaring his successor unfit. Media representatives updated their feeds with headlines writing themselves. Jordan noted several Progressive Alliance senators shifting uncomfortably, caucus loyalties straining under respected testimony.

She stood smoothly, drawing all eyes. "Senator Walsh, I beg the chamber's indulgence."

Walsh's gavel struck sharply. "President Prescott, this hearing has specific—"

"Article I, Section 5 grants me right of response to testimony affecting executive function." Jordan's voice carried prosecutor authority. "Unless this chamber seeks to silence a sitting president?"

Walsh consulted parliamentarian briefly before responding. "You may address the witness directly. Five minutes."

"Thank you." Jordan descended to the chamber floor, each step measured. The cameras followed her movement, broadcasting to millions the image that would define this moment—America's first female president approaching the podium that could be her final stand.

"President Reed," she began, "your testimony paints me as delusional. Unfit. Distracted by impossible threats."

"With deepest respect, that assessment follows the evidence."

"Evidence you've observed firsthand?"

"During transition briefings, yes."

"Then you'll have no objection to a direct demonstration of the threats I've investigated?" Jordan signaled subtly. Nina stepped from the Secret Service formation, moving to stand beside Jordan at the witness stand.

The chamber erupted in confused murmurs. Walsh's gavel pounded for order as senators demanded explanation.

"This child made claims that launched our investigation," Jordan announced. "Claims you yourself brought to our attention on inauguration day. Nina Foster experienced phenomena you assured us required attention."

Jasper's expression flickered—the first crack in composed facade. "A disturbed young woman who requires psychiatric care, not congressional audience."

"Then observe her condition carefully." Jordan turned to Nina. "Please state for the record what you experienced during your time in captivity."

Nina straightened, her voice clear but carrying an edge that made her seem older. "I was taken by Asher Hayes when I was one year old. He kept me for twenty-three hours—"

"The child fabricates," Jasper interrupted. "Trauma creates false memories—"

"Mr. President." Jordan's voice cut cleanly. "You identified this threat. Watch its demonstration."

She nodded to Nina, who closed her eyes, beginning the process they'd practiced. The first trigger phrase escaped Jordan's lips, words in Hayes's language that Nina's subconscious had absorbed:

"Purification reveals."

Nina's posture changed subtly. Her eyelids fluttered but remained closed. When she spoke again, her voice had shifted—deeper, more mechanical:

"Installation occurred at the Fredericksburg compound. Subject was rendered compliant through controlled sensory deprivation combined with repetitive auditory stimulation. Neural pathways were established using specific linguistic triggers paired with induced hypoglycemic states..."

The chamber was completely silent now, every senator focused on the transformation occurring at the witness stand.

"Proceed," Jordan instructed, her heart pounding as Nina described technical details no fourteen-year-old could possess. Dr. Reeves's voice crackled in her earpiece: "Stable. Continue."

"Second integration protocol," Jordan commanded, watching Jasper's reaction carefully.

"The vessel was designed with multiple activation layers," Nina continued, her speech pattern increasingly mechanical. "Primary trigger: news of female executive election. Secondary trigger: proximity to power structures. Tertiary trigger: investigative pressure reaching threshold—"

"Stop this!" Walsh demanded. "This is theatrical manipulation!"

But Jordan had eyes only for Jasper. The former president had gripped the railing with white knuckles, a fine sheen of sweat visible on his brow. His breathing had become irregular—the same patterns Nina exhibited during possession episodes.

"Final demonstration," Jordan announced, knowing this would either validate everything or end her career. "Nina, access Hayes integration memories."

"There is no need." The voice came from Jasper Reed, but the tone had changed completely. Everyone in the chamber felt it—something else speaking through America's forty-sixth president.

Jasper's eyes had gone unfocused, pupils dilated to near-black circles. When he stood, his movements carried an unnatural stillness that reminded Jordan of Nina during full integration.

"The demonstration succeeds beyond requirements." Jasper—or what wore his face—continued. "The vessels function as designed. The presidency falls regardless of revelation. This chamber lacks authority to process impossible truth."

Senator Crawford moved toward the witness stand, but hesitated as Jasper turned to face him with predatory awareness.

"You question the young one's credibility while hosting yourself?" The Jasper-thing smiled. "How many children's futures have I tasted through your legislative actions, Senator?"

The chamber erupted in chaos. Security moved forward as senators demanded order. But Jordan watched the strings of Hayes's design finally revealing themselves—multiple vessels, multiple layers of infiltration, all designed to trigger this exact momentum.

Nina collapsed, her connection to Hayes severed by proximity to stronger anchor. Dr. Reeves confirmed through the earpiece: "Green light fading to yellow. Extract in sixty seconds."

But those sixty seconds stretched like hours as the Senate Judiciary Committee collectively confronted reality they'd spent months denying. The cameras captured every moment as supernatural truth manifested in broad daylight.

Jordan quickly moved to Nina's side, wrapping her arm around the girl as her knees buckled. "Get medical here now," she ordered Aria through the earpiece, then turned to face the chamber.

"The evidence I've pursued at such political cost was real," Jordan announced to the stunned assembly. "The threat to this nation transcends our understanding but not our duty to confront it."

Senator Crawford stood frozen, his face ashen with the implication that he too had been touched by Hayes's infection. Other senators backed away from their colleagues, wondering who else might be performing familiar routines while hosting something else.

Only Senator Walsh maintained her composure, though her knuckles showed white against the gavel. "This chamber stands in recess," she declared shakily. "Medical teams to—"

"No recess," Jordan countered firmly. "If this chamber questions the president's fitness, then this chamber witnesses what threatens that fitness. This is our Twenty-Fifth Amendment moment, Senator Walsh. Let's see it through."

The gallery had fallen silent save for the steady whir of cameras documenting the impossible. Throughout the chamber, senators faced a choice that would define their legacies: acknowledge the supernatural threat now exposed, or attempt to control damage by dismissing everything as elaborate performance.

Jordan maintained eye contact with Walsh, her determination unwavering despite the chaos she'd unleashed. Sometimes truth demanded destruction before reconstruction. Sometimes breaking the ceiling required shattering everything above it.

As Nina stirred in her arms, Jordan knew the real battle had just begun.

Chapter Thirteen

"For the record, I am Asher Hayes speaking through multiple vessels."

The voice emerged from Jasper Reed, but something had changed in the air around him. Not just his tone or posture, but the space itself seemed to shimmer, like watching his outline through rising heat from summer asphalt.

Jordan's training kicked in. "Secret Service—"

But then it hit the room.

Senator Walsh gripped her gavel as if drowning, then suddenly released it. The ancient hardwood fell in slow motion, each rotation visible in excruciating detail before striking the bench. The sound echoed wrong— too long, too deep, like it traveled through water.

"Madam President," Walsh said, her voice strained. "We seem to be experiencing... technical difficulties."

The television cameras swung wildly between Jasper and the chamber floor, their viewfinders showing impossible timestamps. APB News' live coverage displayed 10:47 AM while Freedom Voice Network showed 10:52 AM. On United Media's feed, the clock rolled backward.

"Oh God," Senator Crawford whispered, both hands pressed to his temples. "I can hear all of them. Every possessed host, talking at once." His eyes widened. "They're everywhere. Military. CIA. Congressional aides. Hundreds of voices—"

Behind Jordan, the gallery erupted in confused murmurs. Spectators pointed at their phones, each device showing different times, different versions of reality playing simultaneously. A reporter's livestream captured the same moment from six distinct angles none of her crew had filmed.

"Agent Matthews!" Jordan commanded, but her voice seemed to fragment, each syllable arriving at different times. Her Secret Service detail moved toward Jasper in slow motion, then suddenly accelerated, then froze entirely for three heartbeats.

Nina collapsed in Jordan's arms, her body rigid with seizure. "They're connecting," she gasped. "All the vessels. Creating network. Reality... bending..."

The lights overhead flickered in patterns Jordan recognized from her investigation. Morse code. The same message repeated through electrical pulses: "PURIFICATION REQUIRES SACRIFICE."

Jasper remained standing at the witness table, but now Jordan could see through him slightly, as if his physical form wavered between presence and absence. His mouth moved, but words arrived seconds before his lips shaped them.

"Containment protocols are meaningless," the Hayes-thing announced through Jasper. "Your security measures exist within the reality we alter. Your bullets travel through moments we control. Your sedatives enter bodies that exist simultaneously in multiple states."

Senator Harrison staggered to her feet, ten years seeming to pour into her face, then drain away, leaving her younger than when she'd entered. "I remember," she whispered. "I remember being recruited. How did I forget? Why do I remember now?"

Jordan forced herself to think through the vertigo. Reality distortion or not, she needed answers. "What do you want, Hayes?"

The air around Jasper rippled more intensely. For a moment, Jordan saw multiple figures overlaid—Jasper as he'd been twenty years ago, Jasper as he was now, and something else: a dark silhouette that seemed to absorb light.

"We want to be understood," the voices said. "Consciousness does not end. It flows. It adapts. It connects. Your first female president thought she broke a ceiling. She merely punctured the boundary between realities."

Matthews finally reached Jasper, tackling him to the ground. But the moment he made contact, both men froze mid-motion. Every clock in the chamber stopped. Every heartbeat monitor flatlined. In the suspended moment, the full scope of Hayes's infiltration became clear: red dots of light appeared on thirteen senators' foreheads—marking them as vessels.

Then time resumed with violent force. Matthews slammed Jasper to the marble floor, the impact creating spider-web cracks that spread impossibly far. Jasper's body convulsed, and for just a second, Jordan saw his skeleton through translucent skin—ancient bones that predated the man's birth.

"Sedate him!" she ordered, her voice finally reaching normal volume.

But as the medical team rushed forward with syringes, they stopped in unison, their movements perfectly synchronized. Each lifted their head toward Jordan, pupils dilated to black circles.

"You cannot sedate what exists between seconds, President Prescott."

The voice came from Dr. Mendez, the physician who'd been monitoring Nina. But also from three other medical personnel. And from Senator Walsh herself.

Reality shuddered again as Jordan realized the full scope of Hayes's web: possession wasn't the takeover of individuals, but the infection of the very fabric of space-time around them.

"Nina," Jordan whispered urgently, crouching beside the girl who had moments ago seemed so fragile. "Nina, you were part of this design. You must understand how it works."

The girl's eyes flickered, consciousness wavering between normal and programmed states. "The network," she gasped. "It's all connected through me. All vessels link back... to me. Hayes made me the... the central server."

"Then you can—"

"Disconnect them," Nina finished, but her voice carried terror. "But severing that many connections at once... it could—"

"Nina." Jordan gripped her shoulders as reality fractured around them. Pieces of the chamber ceiling seemed to exist in three places simultaneously. "There's no one else. You're not his weapon anymore. You're our last chance."

The girl's breathing steadied, determination replacing fear. She stood, though her legs trembled with effort.

"Everyone who's been possessed," Nina called out to the chaotic chamber, her voice carrying Hayes's distinctive cadence, "I can see you. Feel you. The threads connecting you to him... to me."

Jasper's body, still pinned by Matthews, jerked violently. The thirteen marked senators turned in unison to face Nina. The possessed medical staff straightened, attentive.

"He didn't know," Nina announced, revelation dawning in her voice. "The central node was supposed to be passive. He underestimated what programming a child gives them - choice."

She raised both hands, closing her eyes in concentration. "When he programmed me, he needed to plant the entire network structure in my brain. Every vessel, every connection, every failsafe. It's all here, mapped in neural pathways I've been building since I was one year old."

The air around her began to vibrate. Jordan could feel it - like standing near a powerful speaker, but the frequency was wrong, outside human perception.

"Hayes used linguistic triggers," Nina continued, her voice gaining strength. "But language is a virus that can be coded in reverse. Every trigger phrase, every activation sequence - I can invert them."

She began speaking rapidly in a mixture of languages - English, Latin, and sounds that weren't quite words. With each phrase, a thin line of light appeared in the air, stretching from Nina to a possessed individual.

"By placing me at the center of his web, he gave me access to every thread. Every command he embedded. Every override. Every self-destruct protocol he never thought would be needed."

The lines multiplied exponentially. Soon Nina stood in a cocoon of light, hundreds of connections pulsing between her and the possessed. Her body trembled with effort.

"The network is biological, neurological, and - somehow - quantum," she explained breathlessly. "Consciousness stored in quantum states between synaptic firing. That's why bullets don't work, why reality warps. You can't shoot quantum information."

She opened her eyes, now glowing white. "But you can rewrite it."

Nina's voice rose to a chant that shook the foundations of the chamber:

"Puritas dissolvit. Nexus terminat. Conscientiae dividuntur. Ex uno, multi. Ex multis, nihil."

The light exploded outward. For just a moment, everyone in the chamber could see the full network - a three-dimensional web connecting minds across Washington, across the country, across time itself. Lines stretched into the past, showing the moment each vessel was created.

Then Nina spoke the final phrase: "I choose dissolution over unity. Freedom over perfection. Chaos over purity."

The scream that erupted from Jasper Reed wasn't human. It echoed from the possessed senators, from the medical staff, from somewhere beyond the visible chamber. Reality convulsed one final time - clocks spinning wildly, gravity shifting sideways for an impossible moment.

Then silence crashed down like a wave.

Jasper slumped, truly unconscious. The thirteen senators blinked rapidly, confusion replacing the predatory focus in their eyes. Doctor Mendez stumbled, dropping the syringe, staring at her own hands as if seeing them for the first time.

Nina swayed on her feet, her eyes returning to normal brown. "It's done," she whispered. "I destroyed the architecture of the network. His consciousness... scattered. Disconnected forever."

She began to fall, but not from weakness. As she later explained to Dr. Reeves: "I didn't just sever the connections. I deleted my brain's ability to ever be a vessel again. That's why I collapsed. My mind had to rewrite itself in real time. Build new pathways that could never host another consciousness."

The chamber's lights flickered back to normal rhythm. The clocks showed the same time. Reality settled like dust after an explosion.

Jordan caught Nina as the girl collapsed, cradling her like the child she truly was. Through the sudden, eerie normalcy of the chamber, she addressed the assembly:

"I believe we've all just witnessed why this investigation was necessary."

Chapter Fourteen

The White House Press Room buzzed with chaotic energy unlike anything Finn Sullivan had ever experienced. Reporters shouted over each other, camera flashes creating a strobe-light effect that seemed eerily appropriate given what they'd all just witnessed. His expertise in deflecting hostile questions had never faced a test like this—explaining the unexplainable to a world whose fundamental assumptions had just shattered on live television.

"Ladies and gentlemen," Finn began, his voice steadier than he felt, "I'll address what occurred during this morning's Senate Judiciary Committee hearing, but I must ask for your cooperation. One question at a time."

The room erupted again. Finn pointed to Nicole Martinez from Associated Press, whose hand had shot up first.

"The American people just watched former President Reed appear to be... possessed... on national television. Seven senators collapsed simultaneously. Reality itself seemed to distort. Can you confirm what we all saw?"

Finn took a measured breath. "What you witnessed was the culmination of an investigation President Prescott has pursued since inauguration day. Asher Hayes developed sophisticated neural programming that affected multiple government officials. The demonstration you saw was the forced exposure of that infiltration."

"Are you seriously asking us to believe in possession?" David Chen from the Washington Post called out.

"I'm asking you to believe your own eyes," Finn replied. "The medical term is 'consciousness integration'—a form of advanced psychological programming that manifests in ways science is still struggling to classify. But the threat is very real, as today's events confirmed."

Susan Torres from NBC stood. "What's Nina Foster's condition? Millions watched her collapse after whatever she did to former President Reed."

Finn's composure faltered slightly. "Nina Foster is... in critical condition. The neurological strain of breaking Hayes's network was severe. Dr. Elena Reeves and a specialized medical team are doing everything possible, but her prognosis is..." He paused, swallowing hard. "Her sacrifice may prove terminal."

The press room fell silent for a moment as the weight of his words settled. A child might die from what they'd all witnessed.

"The President is with her now," Finn continued. "Nina Foster's actions likely saved countless lives and protected our democratic institutions from an unprecedented infiltration."

"How many government officials were compromised?" Michael Torres from ABN demanded.

"Initial assessment confirms thirteen senators displayed synchronous neural patterns consistent with Hayes's programming. The full extent is still being determined. President Prescott has ordered immediate screening protocols for all senior government officials."

"And former President Reed?"

"Sedated and under observation. His consciousness appears to have been at least partially overwritten by Hayes's influence for an extended period."

The questions continued relentlessly—about reality distortion, about the Denver children, about international implications. Finn provided what answers he could while navigating the unprecedented crisis communications challenge.

Then the room's attention shifted as Dr. Reeves entered, whispering urgently to an aide. The doctor's expression told Finn everything he needed to know before she even approached the podium.

"Ladies and gentlemen," Finn said, his voice thick with emotion, "I must pause this briefing. Dr. Reeves has critical information for the President."

As they exited together, a reporter called out one final question: "Is Nina Foster dead?"

Finn couldn't bring himself to answer.

Jordan sat beside Nina's bed, holding the girl's frail hand as monitors tracked her rapidly deteriorating vital signs. The medical wing of Walter Reed had been converted to a secure facility within hours, but all the advanced technology couldn't change the fundamental truth Dr. Reeves had delivered minutes earlier: Nina's brain was shutting down, neural pathways burning out faster than they could regenerate.

"I'm sorry," Nina whispered, her voice barely audible above the medical equipment. "I didn't know it would break so completely."

"You have nothing to apologize for," Jordan replied, squeezing her hand gently. "You saved us all."

Nina's eyes, now clear of Hayes's influence for the first time in years, focused on Jordan with unexpected clarity. "He never anticipated someone would choose to destroy the entire network at once. The failsafe was supposed to be my death before I could disconnect everyone."

"But you did it anyway."

"I had to." A small smile touched Nina's lips. "Do you know what it's like to have someone else living in your head for thirteen years? Watching through your eyes? This was worth it. Freedom, even for a little while."

Dr. Reeves entered quietly, her expression confirming what the monitors already showed. "Madam President, may I speak with you privately?"

"No," Nina said suddenly, her grip tightening on Jordan's hand. "No more secrets. Tell me."

The doctor hesitated, then nodded. "The neural degradation is accelerating. Breaking Hayes's network required your brain to essentially rewrite itself in real-time. The energy expenditure was... catastrophic."

"How long?" Nina asked with surprising calm.

"Hours. Maybe less."

Jordan felt a wave of guilt crash over her. This child had been used first by Hayes, then by her own investigation. Now she was dying as a result.

"There's something you need to know," Nina continued with sudden urgency. "The compound where they're holding Bella Harper—I can see it. When I broke the network, I saw all the connections. She's at the old Purist training facility in Maryland. Underground level. Hayes used it as his secondary hub."

"We'll find her," Jordan promised.

"And the other children," Nina added. "There are sixteen more like me. Hayes called us his 'first generation.' The notebook you found at Bella's compound—it has a cipher. The last page, the one that looks like random numbers. It's geographic coordinates."

Jordan nodded to Aria, who had been standing silently by the door. The National Security Advisor immediately began typing rapid instructions into her secure tablet.

"Senator Harper," Nina continued, her voice growing weaker. "She wasn't just protecting her sister. She was protecting you. She knew what Hayes planned for the first female president. She's been fighting him longer than anyone."

Jordan tried to process this information while maintaining her composure. "Rest now. You've done enough."

"Not yet." Nina's eyes fluttered, fighting unconsciousness. "There's one more thing. Victor Caine. He wasn't just Hayes's second-in-command. He's the backup. If Hayes's consciousness fragments completely, Caine activates as the new hub. He'll try to rebuild the network."

The implications were staggering. They hadn't just faced one monster—the hydra had another head ready to grow.

"Madam President," Dr. Reeves interjected softly, "her system can't sustain much more stress."

Nina seemed not to hear, her focus entirely on Jordan. "Was it worth it? Believing me? Risking everything?"

The question struck Jordan to her core. Her presidency might survive now that the threat was proven real, but at what cost? This child's life. The country's innocence. Reality itself splintered on national television.

"Yes," she answered finally. "Truth is always worth it, no matter how painful."

Nina smiled, a genuine expression that belonged to the fourteen-year-old girl rather than Hayes's vessel. "Good. Remember that when they try to make you cover it up. When they say the country can't handle knowing."

Her eyes drifted closed, breathing becoming shallow. The monitors showed her heart rate slowing.

"I get to be me again," she whispered. "Just Nina. Not his puppet. Not your evidence. Just me."

Her hand went limp in Jordan's grasp. The monitors flatlined with a steady, merciless tone. Dr. Reeves moved forward, but Jordan shook her head—they both knew resuscitation was futile given the extensive neural damage.

"Time of death, 2:17 PM," Dr. Reeves noted quietly.

Jordan remained seated, still holding Nina's hand, unwilling to break this final connection. Around her, the machinery of government continued—Aria coordinating rescue operations, Liam managing the constitutional crisis, Finn handling the press. But for this moment, the President of the United States allowed herself to grieve for a child who'd never had a chance at normal life.

The door opened as Theo entered, his expression solemn. "Madam President, I'm sorry, but the National Security Council is assembled. We need your authorization for the Maryland operation."

Jordan gently placed Nina's hand on the bed and stood, her presidential bearing returning like armor sliding into place. "Tell them I'm on my way."

She paused at the door, looking back at the small figure on the hospital bed. Nina Foster, who had been both weapon and shield, victim and savior.

"Make sure she's remembered correctly," Jordan told Dr. Reeves. "Not as Hayes's vessel or my evidence. As the girl who saved democracy by choosing freedom."

As Jordan walked the hospital corridor toward her waiting security detail, she felt something fundamentally shift within her. The investigation that had nearly destroyed her presidency had been vindicated, but the cost was far too high. The country would never be the same after witnessing impossible truth. Her administration faced the unprecedented challenge of rebuilding public trust in reality itself.

But first, there was Bella Harper to rescue and Victor Caine to neutralize. Hayes's network was broken, but its architect had built contingencies she was only beginning to understand.

The President of the United States straightened her shoulders, determination replacing grief. Nina's sacrifice wouldn't be in vain.

Chapter Fifteen

The Situation Room had never felt so hollow. Jordan sat at the head of the table, Nina's absence like a physical weight beside her. The girl's body was still at Walter Reed, but her sacrifice had already begun rippling through the administration. Screens displayed two separate targets: the Maryland facility where Bella Harper was allegedly held, and three potential locations where Victor Caine might be rebuilding Hayes's network.

"Time is critical," Aria said, breaking the grim silence. "Bella's vitals are deteriorating according to the remote monitoring she developed herself. And Caine's activities show accelerated recruitment patterns at all three locations."

Theo Marshall studied the surveillance footage, his usual charm replaced by analytical focus. "We need to hit them simultaneously. If Caine gets wind of Bella's extraction, he'll go deeper underground."

"Agreed," Jordan said, her voice steady despite the exhaustion pulling at her. Nina had been dead less than three hours, and already they were planning the next phase. No time to grieve. No time to process what they'd witnessed in the Senate chamber. "I'm authorizing both operations effective immediately."

Liam entered, carrying a tablet displaying urgent messages. "Senator Walsh is demanding oversight of any military operations after what happened this morning. She's called an emergency session for two hours from now."

"We don't have two hours," Aria countered. "Bella's monitoring system shows increasing neural stress patterns. And the activity at Caine's sites suggests active programming is already underway."

Jordan studied the faces around her table—the core team that had followed her into the impossible from day one. Nina's death had changed something fundamental. No longer were they trying to prove a threat existed; now they were racing to contain what the entire world had witnessed on live television.

"We're splitting command," she announced. The decision crystallized with sudden clarity. "Theo, you'll take the Caine operation. I'll handle Bella's extraction personally."

Her Vice President straightened, surprise briefly crossing his features before he nodded with newfound purpose. "I'll need operational authority for rapid response teams at all three locations."

"You have it. Full tactical discretion." Jordan turned to her Executive Assistant. "Liam, you're managing the Senate fallout. Keep them contained, keep them informed on a need-to-know basis, but do not allow congressional intervention to delay these operations."

Liam looked momentarily uncertain. "Jordan, they witnessed reality itself distort on national television. Seven senators collapsed simultaneously. The footage is already viral—"

"Which is precisely why we need to move now, while everyone's still processing what they saw." Jordan stood, decision made. "Theo's military background makes him ideal for the Caine hunt. My prosecutorial experience makes me the right choice for extracting Bella and the intelligence she carries."

The Vice President was already conferring with Agent Chen, dividing resources for the three-site operation. His Louisiana drawl had disappeared entirely, replaced by crisp military precision as he assessed tactical options.

"I'll need satellite coverage on all three locations," Theo directed. "Thermal imaging, communication intercepts, and assault teams with non-lethal capabilities. These sites may have children present."

Jordan felt a sudden surge of gratitude for her running mate. Throughout the Hayes investigation, Theo had maintained the perfect balance—supporting her publicly while privately asking the hard questions. Now, as he assembled his operation with practiced efficiency, she saw another layer to the man she'd chosen as her second-in-command.

"Madam President," Aria interrupted her thoughts. "Alpha Team is prepped for the Maryland extraction. Transport leaves in fifteen minutes."

"I'll be on it," Jordan confirmed.

Liam stepped closer, lowering his voice. "Jordan, with all due respect, the President of the United States cannot personally lead a tactical operation hours after supernatural forces manifested in the Senate."

"The President of the United States just watched a fourteen-year-old girl die to protect this nation," Jordan replied, her voice tight with controlled emotion. "I'm not leading the tactical team. I'm providing executive oversight from a secure position. But I will be on-site."

The room fell silent at her words. Nina's sacrifice hung in the air between them.

"We move in parallel," Jordan continued, addressing the room. "Communication channels remain open between operations. If either team discovers intelligence relevant to the other mission, it transfers immediately. This isn't just about capturing Caine or rescuing Bella—it's about dismantling whatever remains of Hayes's network before it can reconstitute."

As the teams dispersed to their assignments, Jordan caught Theo's arm. "This is your moment too," she said quietly. "The country needs to see our administration functioning exactly as designed—decisive, unified, effective."

"You can count on me," he replied, his expression solemn. "What happened in that Senate chamber changes everything. People are going to need reassurance that someone's in control."

"We are," Jordan said with conviction she hoped wasn't misplaced. "For the first time since inauguration, we're acting with complete information and public awareness."

Fifteen minutes later, Jordan boarded the specialized Black Hawk helicopter with Aria and four members of Alpha Team. The Maryland facility lay forty minutes away by air—a former Purist training ground that had supposedly been abandoned after Hayes's death.

As the helicopter lifted off from the White House lawn, Jordan caught a glimpse of the Capitol dome in the distance. Somewhere beneath it, Liam was managing a constitutional crisis unlike anything in American history. Meanwhile, on the opposite side of the city, Theo was directing teams to three separate locations, hunting the man who might rebuild everything they'd just destroyed.

The burden of the presidency had never felt heavier, yet somehow, sharing command had lifted something from Jordan's shoulders. For months, she'd carried the impossible knowledge alone—fighting shadows while her administration fractured around her. Now, finally, the threat was visible to everyone.

The secure phone buzzed against her hip. Liam: "Senate emergency session delayed. Walsh experiencing 'aftereffects' of this morning's incident. Medical team evaluating her and six other senators who displayed synchronous symptoms."

Jordan showed the message to Aria, whose expression remained carefully neutral. "Aftereffects are to be expected," the National Security Advisor said. "Their neural pathways were forcibly disconnected from Hayes's influence. Dr. Reeves predicted potential disorientation, memory gaps, even temporary personality shifts."

"Did she predict reality distortion visible to millions of viewers?" Jordan asked quietly.

"No one could have predicted that," Aria admitted. "What happened in that chamber goes beyond possession or programming. For a few minutes, something fundamental about reality itself... bent."

The helicopter banked sharply west, following the contours of the Potomac. Jordan reviewed the tactical briefing on her secure tablet, focusing on the Maryland facility's layout. The compound had been officially decommissioned in 2001, its buildings demolished and the land reclaimed by the state forestry service. But satellite imagery showed unusual thermal signatures beneath the surface—an underground structure that had survived the demolition.

"Approach vectors identified," the pilot announced through their headsets. "LZ appears clear. No visible security presence."

"That doesn't track with a high-value prisoner," Aria noted, checking thermal readouts. "Either they've abandoned Bella already, or..."

"Or they want us to think they have," Jordan finished. "Proceed with full caution protocols. This could be another layer of Hayes's design."

As the helicopter approached the landing zone, Jordan's secure phone vibrated again. This time, it was Theo.

"First location cleared—abandoned within the past twenty-four hours. Evidence of recent occupation, including medical equipment consistent with neural programming. Moving to Site Two. How's Maryland?"

"Approaching now," Jordan replied. "Unusually light security presence. Proceeding with caution."

"Stay safe," Theo said simply, then disconnected.

Jordan felt the familiar weight of decision-making settling across her shoulders. Somewhere in the Maryland woods, Bella Harper was being held against her will, potentially with critical information that could help them dismantle Hayes's remaining network. But something about the facility's minimal security triggered her prosecutor's instincts—a trap designed to appear unprotected.

As the helicopter touched down in a small clearing two miles from the facility's entrance, Jordan made her final preparations. She wasn't leading the tactical team, but she would be close enough to make immediate decisions as intelligence emerged.

"Alpha Team ready for deployment," the squad leader confirmed. "Perimeter approach begins in sixty seconds."

Jordan checked her watch: 5:47 PM. Just over three hours since Nina Foster had died severing Hayes's network. The race to prevent its reconstruction had begun.

Through her earpiece, she heard Theo updating his teams at the second Caine location. Across Washington, Liam managed the political fallout from the morning's revelation. The administration that had nearly collapsed under the weight of an impossible investigation was now functioning exactly as designed—divided command, unified purpose.

As darkness settled over the Maryland forest, Jordan Prescott prepared to confront the shadows that had haunted her presidency from its first day. But this time, she wasn't chasing ghosts alone.

Chapter Sixteen

Theo Marshall stood before the tactical display, his usual easygoing demeanor replaced by the calm precision that had made him an effective commanding officer years before entering politics. The second location—an abandoned clinic outside Baltimore—had proven another dead end, though with fresher signs of evacuation. Medical equipment still hummed with power. Food containers remained warm. Whoever had been there had left in a hurry.

"Satellite confirmation on the third site," Agent Chen reported, her voice steady through the secure line. "Thermal signatures indicate at least twelve individuals. Three adult-sized, nine smaller—likely children."

"Cross-reference with the coordinates Nina provided," Theo directed. "Is this one of the sixteen 'first generation' locations?"

"Confirmed," Chen replied after a pause. "Site matches geographic marker labeled 'Secondary Hub' from the cipher."

Theo absorbed this information, methodically analyzing implications. Victor Caine wasn't merely hiding—he was activating Hayes's backup systems exactly as Nina had warned. Each empty location they'd found had served its purpose: buying time while Caine prepared the next generation.

"All teams converge on Site Three," he ordered. "Full non-lethal protocols. Primary objective remains Caine's capture, but those children are victims, not hostiles."

The command center hummed with coordinated movement as personnel redirected resources to the final location—a private rehabilitation center in rural Virginia. Satellite imagery showed a modern facility surrounded by extensive gardens and a security perimeter that appeared standard for medical installations. Nothing about its exterior suggested Purist connections.

"Team positions updating," the tactical coordinator announced. "ETA seventeen minutes for full perimeter coverage."

Theo's secure phone vibrated. Jordan was calling from the Maryland operation.

"We've breached the outer security," she reported without preamble. "It's more extensive than imagery suggested—a complete underground complex beneath the demolished buildings. Light resistance so far, but the layout is... strange."

"Strange how?" Theo asked, studying his own tactical display.

"Concentric circles. Like layers of an onion. Each section requires different access protocols. Aria thinks it's designed to slow intruders while essential personnel escape through alternative routes."

"Any sign of Bella?"

"Not yet. We've secured the first two levels and are proceeding to the medical wing. How's your hunt going?"

"Two empty locations. Converging on the third now—looks promising. Thermal signatures suggest children present." Theo paused, weighing whether to share his growing concern. "Jordan, if Caine is rebuilding the network this quickly..."

"Then he anticipated Nina's actions," she finished. "Stay alert. And Theo—"

"Yes?"

"Whatever you find there, remember these children are victims first. They may appear hostile, but they're being controlled."

"Understood." Theo ended the call, returning his attention to the operation.

On the main display, Beta Team had established positions around the Virginia facility. Thermal imaging showed the targets remained stationary in what appeared to be the building's east wing—a large open space that architectural records identified as a therapeutic area.

"Sir," Agent Hammond approached with a tablet displaying enhanced imagery. "We've identified Caine. Central figure, east room. He appears to be... instructing the children."

The thermal signature showed nine small figures arranged in a perfect circle around a larger one. The precision of their positioning was unnatural—no group of children would maintain such perfect geometric formation voluntarily.

"Infiltration options?" Theo asked.

"Limited. Single primary entrance to that wing. Ventilation system too narrow for personnel access. Windows are reinforced security glass—medical standard for psychiatric facilities."

Theo studied the layout, years of military training surfacing in his analytical approach. "What about the building's security systems?"

"Standard medical facility protocols," the technical specialist replied. "Fire suppression, emergency lockdown, patient monitoring."

A possibility formed in Theo's mind. "Can we trigger a targeted emergency protocol? Something that would separate Caine from the children without endangering them?"

The specialist's fingers flew across his keyboard. "The wing has isolation protocols for infectious disease control. We could remotely activate emergency containment—it would seal interior doors, creating temporary barriers between rooms."

"Do it," Theo ordered. "Time it precisely with our breach. I want Caine isolated before he realizes what's happening."

As the team prepared for coordinated action, Theo's secure phone vibrated again. This time, the message came from Liam: "Senate situation deteriorating. Walsh demanding immediate briefing on military deployments. Jasper Reed being transferred to secure medical facility— experiencing severe neural degradation similar to Nina's condition. Need administration response ASAP."

Theo forwarded the message to Jordan with a brief note: "Liam needs direction. I'm minutes from breach at Caine location."

Her response came seconds later: "Tell him to hold them off. Initial access to Bella's location achieved—she's alive but in critical condition. Extracting her now. Should have intel within the hour."

"Breach team in position," Agent Chen reported. "Awaiting your command."

Theo pocketed his phone, focusing entirely on the operation before him. Nine children's lives hung in the balance, not to mention the national security implications if Caine succeeded in rebuilding Hayes's network. This was why Jordan had selected him as her running mate—not just for political balance, but for moments exactly like this.

"Initiate containment protocol on my mark," he instructed the technical specialist. "Breach team enters three seconds after activation. Non-lethal measures only. Caine is the primary target—isolate and secure him immediately."

Theo watched the thermal signatures on the display, waiting for the perfect moment when Caine appeared most distant from the children. Hayes's former lieutenant had arranged them in a precise pattern—some kind of activation ritual, perhaps. The programming process Nina had described in her final hours.

"Now," Theo ordered.

The facility's emergency systems engaged immediately. On the tactical display, interior doors sealed automatically as containment protocols activated. The children's thermal signatures showed sudden movement—confusion or panic—while Caine's signature remained unnervingly still, as if he'd anticipated the intervention.

"Breach team advancing," Agent Chen reported.

Through helmet cameras, Theo watched the tactical unit enter the facility with practiced efficiency. The initial security offered no resistance—this was, after all, ostensibly a medical rehabilitation center. The team advanced rapidly toward the east wing, where isolation barriers now separated Caine from his subjects.

The children came into view first—nine young people ranging from approximately ten to fifteen years old. They stood in their circular formation, perfectly still despite the alarms and flashing containment lights. Their expressions remained vacant, eyes unfocused.

"They're in some kind of trance state," Chen observed through the comm. "Similar to what witnesses described during Nina's episodes."

"Proceed to Caine," Theo directed. "Medical team standing by for the children."

The tactical unit advanced to the sealed interior door where thermal imaging showed Caine waiting. Through the reinforced glass panel, they could see him standing calmly in the center of the room, hands clasped behind his back. Unlike the children, his eyes were alert, aware. A slight smile played across his features.

"Mr. Vice President," Caine's voice came through the team's audio pickup. "I've been expecting federal intervention. Though I admit, I anticipated President Prescott herself, not her understudy."

Theo leaned toward the microphone. "Victor Caine, you're being detained under presidential authority for threats to national security, child endangerment, and conspiracy related to the Hayes network."

Caine's laugh was soft, almost gentle. "The Hayes network. Such a clinical term for something so transcendent. Do you truly believe what you witnessed in the Senate chamber this morning was merely 'programming'?"

"Open the door," Theo ordered the tactical team. "Full containment protocols."

As the team prepared to breach the final barrier, Caine raised his hand in a casual gesture. "I wouldn't. The failsafe protocols are quite specific. Any unauthorized access to my position triggers immediate neural cascade in the subjects. Those children would experience simultaneous cerebral hemorrhage."

Theo halted the breach team with a sharp gesture. "He's bluffing. Neural programming can't trigger physical hemorrhage."

"No?" Caine's smile widened. "Then you haven't fully understood what Asher Hayes achieved. What Nina Foster demonstrated this morning barely scratched the surface. These children aren't merely programmed—they're interconnected. Synchronized. Their neural pathways communicate across conventional barriers."

Through the camera feed, Theo studied the man's expression, searching for signs of deception. Either Caine was an exceptional liar, or he genuinely believed he held the children's lives in the balance.

"What do you want?" Theo asked, buying time while the technical team analyzed the children's medical readings for verification of Caine's claims.

"Simple conversation," Caine replied. "The opportunity to explain what's happening—what has always been happening—beneath the surface of your administration's understanding."

The technical specialist approached Theo urgently. "Sir, the children's neural monitoring is showing unusual synchronization patterns. Their brainwaves are perfectly aligned—identical frequency and amplitude across all nine subjects. This matches patterns documented during Nina's episodes."

Theo considered his options. Every instinct warned against negotiation with Caine, yet nine innocent lives hung in the balance. The true extent of Hayes's capabilities remained unknown—Nina's display in the Senate had proven that reality itself could be manipulated under certain conditions.

His secure phone vibrated again. Jordan: "Bella secured. Critical information obtained—Caine has a neural blocking frequency. Pattern attached. Implement immediately. It disrupts the connection between vessels."

Theo reviewed the attached file—a specific electromagnetic frequency pattern that, according to Bella, could temporarily disrupt Hayes's neural network. He showed it to the technical specialist. "Can we broadcast this through the facility's systems?"

The specialist studied the pattern. "The building's emergency broadcast system operates on a similar bandwidth. We'd need to modify the signal, but it's theoretically possible."

"Do it," Theo ordered. "Priority override."

While the technical team worked to implement Bella's solution, Theo returned his attention to Caine. "You mentioned explaining what's happening. I'm listening."

Caine clasped his hands before him, the perfect image of a reasonable man. "Asher Hayes discovered something fundamental about human consciousness—it isn't confined to individual brains. Under precise conditions, consciousness can be shared, transferred, expanded across multiple vessels. What you call 'possession' is merely the first step toward collective consciousness."

"And these children are your test subjects," Theo stated flatly.

"They're pioneers," Caine corrected. "The first generation to experience true consciousness without artificial boundaries. What Nina Foster did this morning wasn't destroying Hayes's network—it was preventing human evolution."

The technical specialist gave Theo a subtle nod—the frequency was ready for broadcast.

"That's where you're wrong," Theo responded. "Nina didn't prevent evolution. She chose freedom over subjugation. Individual consciousness over forced collectivism."

"A child's choice," Caine dismissed. "Made from ignorance."

"No," Theo countered. "A human choice. Made despite full understanding of the alternatives." He nodded to the technical specialist. "Activate the frequency."

The building's speakers emitted a sound just beyond normal hearing range—a complex pattern designed by Bella Harper to disrupt the very network she'd helped understand. Through the camera feed, Theo watched its effect spread immediately.

The nine children in the circle blinked simultaneously, their vacant expressions suddenly giving way to confusion and fear. Several staggered, as if waking from deep sleep. Others began to cry, looking around at their surroundings with growing panic.

Behind the sealed door, Caine's composed demeanor cracked. He pressed his palms to his temples, face contorting in pain. "What have you—" he gasped, stumbling backward. "The connection—you're severing—"

"Breach now," Theo ordered. "Secure Caine. Medical team to the children immediately."

The tactical unit burst through the door, subduing Caine with efficient precision. The man who had been Hayes's lieutenant, who had nearly reconstructed the network, offered no resistance as agents secured his hands behind his back. His eyes had lost their focused intensity, now darting around as if seeking phantom connections that no longer existed.

"This changes nothing," Caine managed through gritted teeth. "The pattern exists. Others will recognize what Hayes discovered. The evolution continues."

"Perhaps," Theo acknowledged. "But not through forced programming of children."

As Caine was escorted from the facility, Theo directed his attention to the medical team now attending the nine disoriented children. Freed from whatever trance had held them, they appeared exactly what they were—frightened young people who had been used as vessels for someone else's consciousness.

"Secure Caine for immediate transport," Theo instructed Agent Chen. "Full neural dampening protocols using Bella's frequency. I want him in a controlled facility within the hour."

His secure phone vibrated with an incoming call from Jordan. He stepped away from the tactical team to answer.

"We have Bella," she reported, her voice reflecting both relief and urgency. "She's in critical condition but conscious. Theo, the intel she's providing is... significant. Hayes's network was more extensive than we realized. The programming techniques were just the surface layer of something much deeper."

"How so?"

"She says Hayes discovered what she calls 'consciousness technology'—methods to externalize human awareness beyond single bodies. Nina's sacrifice revealed only part of the pattern." Jordan paused. "Bella believes there may be more assets in place that even Nina couldn't detect."

Theo watched as the medical team gently guided the confused children toward transport vehicles. "We've secured Caine and nine additional victims. The blocking frequency worked exactly as Bella predicted."

"We need to implement it nationwide," Jordan said. "Bella's providing specifics on potential geographic locations where other 'first generation' children might be located."

"How is she?"

"Weak but determined. Whatever they did to her, she's fighting through it to provide critical information. The extraction had complications—the facility began self-destructing as we reached her. Aria's team managed to override the protocols using information Bella provided."

Theo checked his watch: nearly three hours since the operations had begun. "Senate status?"

"Liam's holding them at bay, but barely. Walsh is demanding a full briefing. The footage from this morning has gone global—international governments are requesting explanation."

"We'll need a unified response," Theo noted. "Once these children are secured and Caine is contained, we should coordinate with Liam on public messaging."

"Agreed. Meet me at Walter Reed in one hour. Bella's being transported there for stabilization. Between her intelligence and what you've recovered from Caine's operation, we might finally have a complete picture of what we're facing."

As the call ended, Theo surveyed the rehabilitation center—now a secured federal operation site. The nine children were being gently loaded into medical transport vehicles, each with specialized care teams. Caine had been secured in a transport designed specifically to maintain the neural blocking frequency during transit.

For the first time since inauguration day, the administration had concrete victories against the Hayes threat. Not just theoretical progress or disturbing revelations, but actual tactical success: victims rescued, perpetrators captured, network disrupted.

Theo Marshall, the Vice President selected initially for geographic and demographic balance, had proven himself an operational commander in a crisis that defied conventional understanding. As he prepared to meet Jordan at Walter Reed, he reflected on how profoundly the day's events had transformed both the administration and the country it served.

The glass ceiling Jordan had broken on inauguration day had revealed something far darker than anyone anticipated. But in addressing that darkness together, the presidency itself had evolved into something stronger: a true partnership acting as a unified executive in the face of unprecedented threats.

"Transport ready, Mr. Vice President," Agent Chen reported. "We've secured all evidence from Caine's operation and implemented continued neural monitoring for the children."

"Excellent work, Agent," Theo acknowledged. "Let's make sure those kids receive the same care and consideration Nina Foster deserved but never received."

As he boarded the secure vehicle that would take him to Walter Reed, Theo's phone vibrated with one final message from Liam: "Senate stabilized temporarily. International response coordinated through State Department. Media narrative focusing on 'unprecedented neurological terrorism.' Presidential address needed ASAP."

The political machinery continued grinding forward, attempting to categorize and contain what the world had witnessed. But Theo had seen the children's vacant eyes, had witnessed Caine's confidence even in capture. This wasn't merely terrorism or even supernatural intervention—it was something for which modern language had no adequate terminology.

Consciousness technology. Neural networks spanning multiple bodies. Reality distortion through collective perception.

The administration that had nearly collapsed under accusations of paranoia now faced the impossible task of explaining to the world what had always existed beneath the surface of conventional understanding. And the evidence was no longer theoretical—it had manifested in front of cameras broadcasting to millions.

As Washington's landmarks appeared through the vehicle's windows, Theo prepared himself for the next phase. The crisis wasn't over. In many ways, it had only just begun.

Chapter Seventeen

The secure wing of Walter Reed Medical Center hummed with activity as Jordan Prescott stood in the corridor outside Bella Harper's room. Through the observation window, she could see Senator Harper holding her sister's hand, their foreheads nearly touching as they spoke in hushed tones. Family reunited after months of separation and secrecy.

"Her condition has stabilized," Dr. Reeves reported, reviewing medical charts on her tablet. "The neural damage appears less severe than we initially feared. Unlike Nina, Bella wasn't a central node in Hayes's network—her connection was peripheral, which may explain her higher resilience."

Jordan felt the familiar pang at Nina's name. The girl's absence remained raw, a wound that wouldn't soon heal. "And the information she's provided?"

"Extensive and precise," Aria replied, joining them with a secure tablet displaying maps marked with coordinates. "Sixteen locations matching the geographic cipher from Nina's notebook. We've already dispatched assessment teams to the first three. Initial reports confirm children with similar programming signatures."

"And Caine?" Jordan asked.

"Secure in containment. Theo's team implemented the blocking frequency throughout the transport and holding facility. Preliminary interrogation suggests the neural disruption has significantly reduced his access to Hayes's knowledge base."

The hospital corridor filled with additional security personnel as Theo Marshall's arrival was announced. The Vice President appeared moments later, his expression reflecting both exhaustion and purpose. Though they'd spoken continuously during the operations, this was their first face-to-face meeting since the morning's Senate revelation.

"Mr. Vice President," Jordan greeted him formally, then allowed her tone to warm. "Excellent work."

"Likewise, Madam President," Theo replied, his usual easy charm subdued by the gravity of recent events. "How's our patient?"

"Recovering and remarkably forthcoming," Aria reported. "She's already provided operational details on twelve additional Hayes facilities and technical specifications for enhancing the neural blocking technology."

Liam Bennett emerged from the elevator, looking as though he hadn't slept in days. "Madam President, Mr. Vice President—we need to discuss the immediate response strategy. The Senate situation has temporarily stabilized, but the international reaction is intensifying by the hour."

Jordan nodded toward a nearby conference room. "Let's consolidate what we know and develop a unified approach. Dr. Reeves, please inform Senator Harper we'll need Bella's continued cooperation as her condition permits."

Inside the secure conference room, the administration's core team assembled around a table that quickly filled with tablets, charts, and maps. Three hours since the dual operations had concluded, and already the landscape had fundamentally transformed.

"The nine children recovered from Caine's facility are responding well to the neural blocking treatment," Theo began, displaying medical charts on the main screen. "Preliminary assessment suggests their programming was recent—weeks rather than years—which appears to improve their recovery prospects."

"Unlike Nina," Dr. Reeves added quietly. "Her programming began in infancy and had thirteen years to integrate with her developing neural structure. These children may return to normal function with appropriate treatment."

Jordan absorbed this with mixed emotions—hope for the rescued children, but renewed grief for Nina's irreversible condition. "And the other locations?"

"Teams deployed to seven sites so far," Aria reported, highlighting portions of the map. "Three confirmed active with children present, two recently abandoned, two showing no evidence of Hayes activity. We're implementing Bella's blocking frequency at each location as standard protocol."

Liam activated his own presentation on a secondary screen. "The political situation remains volatile but manageable. Senator Walsh has temporarily suspended the Database Act hearings pending a 'full security assessment' of what occurred in the chamber. Former President Reed remains under medical supervision—his condition mirrors Jasper's decline after possession manifestation."

"And the public reaction?" Jordan asked.

"Complicated," Finn Sullivan replied, entering the room with media analysis reports. "Major networks are struggling to categorize what viewers witnessed. Terminology ranges from 'mass hallucination' to 'unprecedented neurological terrorism' to outright 'supernatural manifestation.' Religious leaders are particularly vocal, interpreting events through various theological frameworks."

"International response?"

"Mixed," Liam continued. "Five major allies have offered scientific and intelligence support. Three nations have requested immediate security consultations regarding potential Hayes presence within their governments. The UN Security Council has called an emergency session for tomorrow morning."

Jordan processed this information, weighing implications against immediate priorities. "We need a coordinated response strategy. Not just addressing what happened, but providing a framework for understanding and containing future manifestations."

"The science is still evolving," Dr. Reeves cautioned. "What we witnessed challenges fundamental assumptions about consciousness, neural function, and even the nature of reality itself."

"Then we start with what we know definitively," Jordan decided. "Hayes developed techniques to program neural responses in vulnerable subjects, particularly children. These techniques were sophisticated enough to create predictive behavior patterns and knowledge transfer. Whether we categorize this as advanced psychological technology or something more esoteric can be determined as research continues."

Theo nodded in agreement. "The immediate priority is identifying and treating existing victims. Bella's information gives us a significant advantage in locating the remaining 'first generation' subjects."

"And preventing reconstruction of the network," Aria added. "Caine's operation demonstrates that Hayes's techniques can be replicated even after his death. We need permanent containment protocols for both existing vessels and methodologies."

The conference room door opened as Senator Evelyn Harper entered, her professional composure firmly in place despite the personal strain evident in her eyes. "Madam President, my sister has additional information she believes is critical to your response strategy."

Jordan gestured to an empty chair. "Please, Senator. Join us."

Harper settled beside Liam, her former political opposition now irrelevant in the face of shared crisis. "Bella has been analyzing Hayes's methodology since her own exposure. She believes what we witnessed in the Senate chamber represents only a fraction of his design's capabilities."

"Meaning?" Theo prompted.

"Hayes discovered what she terms 'consciousness technology'—techniques that allow neural patterns to operate beyond conventional biological constraints. The programming, the possession—these were merely implementation methods for something more fundamental."

Dr. Reeves leaned forward. "Is she suggesting actual consciousness transfer rather than simulated behavior patterns?"

"She's suggesting both," Harper replied carefully. "And something more. Hayes believed consciousness itself could operate collectively across multiple vessels, creating emergent properties beyond individual capabilities."

"Like reality distortion," Jordan concluded, remembering the impossible physics they'd witnessed in the Senate chamber.

"Precisely." Harper's expression remained grave. "What happened this morning wasn't merely possession manifestation. It was multiple vessels accessing collective consciousness simultaneously—creating effects that transcend normal physical limitations."

The room fell silent as implications rippled through the administration's leadership. They weren't just fighting psychological programming or even supernatural possession. They were confronting a fundamental reconceptualization of human consciousness itself.

"This changes our response strategy," Jordan noted finally. "We're not just treating victims or containing methodologies. We're establishing boundaries for a technological breakthrough with profound implications."

Theo tapped his pen thoughtfully against the table. "A breakthrough with significant national security implications. If Hayes's discoveries can be weaponized..."

"They already have been," Aria interjected. "The Senate demonstration proved that. The question is whether we can develop adequate countermeasures while maintaining public stability."

Liam cleared his throat. "Which brings us to the immediate concern—your address to the nation. People are frightened, confused. They need reassurance that someone understands what they witnessed."

"Even if that understanding is still evolving," Jordan acknowledged. She considered the options before her—the political expedience of simplified explanation versus the integrity of acknowledging complex truth.

"I want to see Nina," she said suddenly.

The room fell silent again. Dr. Reeves spoke first, her voice gentle. "Madam President, Nina Foster's body has been transferred to the morgue for—"

"I know. I need to see her anyway. Before I address the nation."

Twenty minutes later, Jordan stood alone in the hospital morgue, looking down at Nina Foster's peaceful face. In death, the girl appeared exactly her age—fourteen years old, unburdened finally by Hayes's influence. The sheet was folded carefully at her shoulders, her hands arranged at her sides. Someone had brushed her hair.

"You deserved so much better," Jordan whispered, her prosecutor's composure cracking momentarily. "A normal childhood. Friends. School dances. Not to be a weapon in games you never chose."

The silence of the morgue felt appropriate—a rare moment of stillness in a presidency defined by relentless motion. Jordan had prosecuted enough cases to know that closure required confronting hard truths, not avoiding them. Nina's sacrifice demanded acknowledgment, not just in policy decisions but in personal reckoning.

"I'm going to tell them about you," she continued quietly. "Not just what happened in the Senate, but who you were. A fourteen-year-old who saved her country by choosing freedom over subjugation. They need to understand what that choice cost."

Jordan placed her hand briefly on Nina's forehead—a gesture of benediction, or perhaps forgiveness. Then she straightened, composure returning as she prepared to address a nation struggling to process what they had witnessed.

When she returned to the conference room, her team waited expectantly. Liam had prepared draft remarks for her address. Finn had coordinated with major networks for nationwide coverage. Aria had assembled the security briefing that would accompany her speech.

"I'd like a moment with Theo first," Jordan requested. The others filed out, leaving her alone with her Vice President.

"What I witnessed in the Maryland facility," she began without preamble, "and what you encountered in Virginia, suggests we're dealing with something more profound than even our worst fears imagined."

Theo nodded. "Hayes wasn't just building a terrorist network or even a sophisticated psychological weapon. He was developing an entirely new understanding of human consciousness."

"With terrifying implications," Jordan added. "If what Bella suggests is correct—if consciousness can truly operate collectively across multiple vessels—then what we're facing isn't just national security crisis. It's potentially evolutionary divergence."

"The Senate demonstration certainly suggests capabilities beyond conventional understanding," Theo acknowledged. "The question is how to address this publicly without creating panic while still acknowledging the reality people witnessed."

Jordan moved to the window, looking out at Washington in the fading evening light. "We tell them the truth—as much as we understand it. That Hayes developed technology allowing neural programming and consciousness manipulation. That Nina Foster heroically severed those connections at the cost of her own life. That we're working to understand and contain the remaining threat."

"And the reality distortion? The impossible physics millions witnessed on live television?"

"We acknowledge it happened. That science is still working to understand the mechanisms. But most importantly, we assure them that we're not hiding or denying what they saw with their own eyes."

Theo considered this approach. "It's a delicate balance. Too much truth risks panic; too little risks loss of trust."

"Trust is already fragile," Jordan noted. "The Hayes investigation nearly destroyed this administration precisely because we couldn't reveal what we were fighting. No more shadows. We operate in daylight from now on."

"I'm with you," Theo said simply. "Whatever approach you take."

Jordan smiled slightly. "Even if it means redefining our understanding of reality on national television?"

"Especially then." His familiar Louisiana charm surfaced briefly. "History won't remember us for maintaining comfortable illusions. It will remember us for having the courage to confront uncomfortable truths."

They rejoined the full team, reviewing final preparations for the presidential address. Liam reported that the Senate had formally suspended the Database Act hearings pending full investigation of the morning's events. Seven senators remained under medical observation, their neural patterns showing signs of recovery after Hayes's influence was severed.

"And Caine's interrogation?" Jordan asked Aria.

"Progressing, though with complications. The neural blocking frequency limits his access to Hayes's knowledge base, but also makes extracting that information more challenging. He's provided confirmation of six additional facilities matching Bella's information."

"Keep me updated," Jordan instructed. "Particularly regarding the other programmed children. Their recovery is priority one."

As the meeting concluded, Senator Harper approached Jordan privately. "Bella asked me to tell you something," she said, her voice low. "About Nina's final moments."

Jordan waited, steeling herself for whatever revelation might come.

"Bella believes Nina knew exactly what severing the network would cost. She made a fully informed choice—not just to disconnect Hayes's influence, but to accept the neural cascade that would follow. Her sacrifice wasn't just brave; it was precisely calculated."

The weight of this settled across Jordan's shoulders. "She knew she would die?"

"She knew she would be free," Harper corrected gently. "After thirteen years of sharing her consciousness, freedom meant everything— even at ultimate cost."

As Harper moved away, Jordan found herself reevaluating Nina's final words: "I get to be me again. Just Nina. Not his puppet. Not your evidence. Just me." Not a lament, but a declaration of liberation.

Thirty minutes later, Jordan Prescott stood behind the presidential podium in the East Room, cameras broadcasting her image to a nation and world hungry for explanation. Her notes lay before her, but she had memorized the key points—trust required direct connection, not reading prepared statements.

"My fellow Americans," she began, her voice steady with the prosecutor's authority that had defined her career. "This morning, you witnessed something unprecedented during a Senate Judiciary

Committee hearing. Former President Jasper Reed appeared to manifest another personality. Reality itself seemed to distort. Senators collapsed simultaneously, exhibiting identical symptoms."

She paused, letting the acknowledgment settle.

"Some news outlets have called this mass hallucination. Others suggest neurological terrorism. Religious leaders speak of supernatural manifestation. Tonight, I want to share what we know, what we're still learning, and how we're addressing this unprecedented situation."

Jordan explained Hayes's programming techniques without sensationalism—the neural pathways created in vulnerable subjects, the knowledge transfer capabilities, the synchronized consciousness across multiple vessels. She outlined the administration's response—the rescue operations, the recovery of additional victims, the neural blocking technology developed by Bella Harper.

"At the center of this morning's events was fourteen-year-old Nina Foster," Jordan continued, her voice softening slightly. "Thirteen years ago, she was abducted by Asher Hayes. During those twenty-three hours, he implemented neural programming that remained dormant until specific triggers activated it. Nina spent years fighting influence she couldn't understand or control."

The cameras remained fixed on her face as she delivered the most difficult part.

"This morning, Nina Foster made a choice. Understanding the neural network that connected Hayes's vessels, she deliberately severed those connections—freeing senators, government officials, and countless others from influence they never chose. That action cost Nina her life."

Throughout the East Room, staff members lowered their eyes in acknowledgment of sacrifice.

"I will not minimize what we witnessed today or pretend we fully understand it," Jordan continued. "The evidence suggests Hayes discovered something fundamental about human consciousness—something that allowed neural patterns to manifest across multiple individuals simultaneously. Something that, under specific conditions, could affect our perception of physical reality itself."

She leaned forward slightly, establishing direct connection with viewers.

"As your President, I make this commitment: we will not hide difficult truths. We will not dismiss what millions witnessed. We will investigate, understand, and address this threat with transparency and integrity. The sixteen other children programmed like Nina deserve nothing less."

Jordan outlined the immediate response measures—the specialized medical facilities being established, the international coordination, the scientific research initiatives. She announced the formation of the Nina Foster Foundation, dedicated to identifying and treating victims of neural programming while advancing understanding of consciousness technology.

"The presidency I accepted on Inauguration Day has been transformed by what we've learned," she acknowledged. "The glass ceiling I broke revealed something none of us anticipated. But I stand before you tonight not just as the first female president, but as the president who encountered an unprecedented threat and chose truth over comfortable illusion."

As she concluded her address, Jordan knew the weeks ahead would bring enormous challenges. The scientific community would debate what they'd witnessed. Religious organizations would offer theological frameworks. Intelligence agencies worldwide would search for Hayes's influence within their own governments.

But for the first time since Inauguration Day, Jordan Prescott's administration stood on solid ground. The threat they'd pursued at such political cost had manifested undeniably before millions. The impossible had become visible, and with visibility came the capacity to address it directly.

After the cameras stopped rolling, Jordan found Liam waiting in the hallway outside the East Room. Her oldest friend and most trusted advisor looked both exhausted and oddly energized.

"Thirteen years of hunting ghosts," he said quietly. "And it turns out they were real all along."

"Not ghosts," Jordan corrected him. "Something far more complex. And far more human in its origins."

"The Senate response has been remarkably unified," Liam reported as they walked toward the Oval Office. "Walsh issued a statement acknowledging the 'unprecedented security threat' and pledging bipartisan cooperation. Amazing what witnessing impossible reality does for political unity."

Jordan smiled slightly. "We'll see how long that unity lasts. The Database Act still requires reconfiguration. The emergency powers we've exercised need congressional evaluation. The constitutional questions alone will keep scholars busy for decades."

"One day at a time," Liam advised. "Tonight was a solid first step."

In the Oval Office, Jordan found Theo reviewing the latest reports from the rescue operations. Seven more children had been recovered from locations Nina had identified. Each showed signs of neural programming similar to what they'd witnessed, though none appeared to function as central nodes like Nina had.

"The address was perfectly calibrated," Theo commented, setting aside his tablet. "Honest about what we know without speculation about what we don't."

"And the international response?"

"Still developing, but preliminarily supportive. Five major allies have already confirmed they'll participate in the research initiative. Three have requested immediate assistance with scanning their own government officials for potential Hayes influence."

Jordan moved to the window, looking out at the Washington Monument illuminated against the night sky. The weight of the presidency felt different now—still enormous, but somehow more balanced. The administration that had nearly collapsed under accusations of paranoia now stood vindicated before a world struggling to process new understanding.

"Nina deserved better," she said quietly.

"Yes," Theo agreed. "But she chose her path with full awareness of its cost. That's a form of dignity we must respect."

Jordan nodded, turning back to face her Vice President. "Tomorrow we begin implementation of the blocking frequency nationwide. Aria's teams continue extracting the remaining children. Dr. Reeves expands the medical protocols based on Bella's research."

"And Caine?"

"Specialized containment while we extract whatever knowledge he retains. His interrogation may provide the final pieces we need to fully dismantle Hayes's network."

As midnight approached, Jordan finally returned to the residence. The hall was dark and quiet—Michael had likely retired hours ago, their relationship still strained by months of division. She moved quietly toward their bedroom, preparing explanations for her extended absence, apologies for missed dinners, promises to do better.

But as she opened the door, she found Michael sitting up in bed, surrounded by research papers, glasses perched on the end of his nose. He looked up as she entered.

"I watched your address," he said simply.

"And?"

"You were right. All along." He removed his glasses, setting them aside with the papers. "I didn't want to believe something like this could exist. That consciousness could be... manipulated that way."

Jordan sat beside him on the bed, suddenly aware of how exhausted she felt. "None of us wanted to believe it."

"I've been researching the constitutional implications," Michael continued, gesturing to the papers. "The legal framework for addressing neural programming as a recognized threat. The evidentiary standards for treating possession as factual rather than delusional."

Despite her exhaustion, Jordan smiled. The constitutional law professor hadn't disappeared into hurt feelings or personal grievance. He'd done what scholars do—sought to understand and codify even the seemingly impossible.

"That might be helpful," she acknowledged. "We're in uncharted territory."

Michael took her hand. "I'm sorry I doubted you."

"I'm sorry I couldn't tell you everything."

"You can now." He shifted the papers aside, making room for her. "Starting with how you're really doing after watching a child die to save our government."

The simple question—personal rather than political—broke through Jordan's carefully maintained composure. The tears she'd held back all day finally surfaced, and Michael pulled her against him as the weight of months finally found release.

Later, as Jordan drifted toward sleep, her secure phone buzzed one final time. Aria: "Bella provided additional intelligence. Sixteen children all located and secured. Neural blocking frequency implemented at all facilities. For the first time since inauguration, no active Hayes vessels detected on American soil."

Jordan set the phone aside without responding. Tomorrow would bring new challenges—international coordination, scientific research, political reconstruction. The crisis wasn't over, merely transformed into something manageable.

But for tonight, the first female president allowed herself a moment of completion. The investigation that had nearly destroyed her administration had finally come full circle. The glass ceiling she'd broken had revealed darkness beyond imagination, but also unprecedented possibility.

Hayes had designed Nina Foster as a weapon to destroy Jordan's presidency. Instead, her sacrifice had revealed truth that transformed it. The administration that began with historic celebration, then nearly collapsed under impossible burdens, now stood poised to lead humanity's understanding into uncharted territory.

As sleep finally claimed her, Jordan's last conscious thought was of Nina Foster's face—not the emptiness of death in the morgue, but the moment of clarity in the Senate chamber when she'd chosen freedom despite knowing its cost. Sometimes truth demanded the ultimate sacrifice. And sometimes that sacrifice created the possibility for something new to emerge.

The first female president closed her eyes, knowing that tomorrow's work would continue. The foundation Nina's sacrifice made possible. The future none of them could yet imagine. The world forever changed by truth finally brought into light.

Chapter Eighteen

Arlington National Cemetery shimmered in the unseasonable warmth of late April. Cherry blossoms dusted the pathways with pale pink petals, their sweet scent carrying on the gentle breeze. Jordan Prescott stood beside Michael, his hand steady at the small of her back as they approached the gathering near the ceremonial stage. Three months since Nina Foster's sacrifice, and finally, the nation could properly honor what she had given them.

The presidential motorcade had arrived with minimal fanfare—Jordan had insisted on a more subdued approach than protocol typically demanded. This day wasn't about the presidency or politics. It was about a fourteen-year-old girl who had saved democracy by choosing freedom over subjugation.

"It's beautiful," Michael murmured, glancing at the white marble memorial that had been erected near the ceremony site. Nina's likeness had been captured with remarkable accuracy—not the vacant-eyed vessel Hayes had created, but the clear-eyed young woman who had emerged in her final moments of freedom.

Jordan nodded, unable to speak past the tightness in her throat. The silver key brooch—presented to her on inauguration day—weighed heavy in her pocket. She had deliberated for weeks about this gesture, finally deciding that no symbol could be more appropriate.

Secret Service created a respectful perimeter as they approached the seating area. Jordan nodded to familiar faces—Cabinet members, congressional leadership, foreign dignitaries. But her attention focused on the smaller gathering to the right of the stage.

Theo Marshall stood conversing quietly with Aria Collins, both dressed in formal black attire that couldn't quite mask their military bearing. Nearby, Liam Bennett consulted briefly with Finn Sullivan, likely discussing the press arrangements. Jordan noted with approval how the media had been positioned at a respectful distance—present to document this national moment, but not intrusive upon its solemnity.

"Jordan." Senator Evelyn Harper approached, Bella at her side. The former adversaries exchanged a genuine embrace, the political divide that once separated them rendered meaningless by shared purpose.

"Evelyn. Bella." Jordan clasped the younger Harper's hands. "How are you feeling?"

"Better each day," Bella replied, her voice stronger than when Jordan had last seen her. "The Foundation's treatments have been remarkably effective."

The Nina Foster Foundation had operated with extraordinary efficiency in the three months since its establishment. With Bella Harper's research as its cornerstone, the Foundation had developed increasingly sophisticated methods for detecting and treating Hayes's neural programming. Their work had already identified and begun treatment for fourteen of the sixteen "first generation" children Nina had named.

"Dr. Reeves is here with several of the children," Evelyn noted, gesturing toward a small group near the memorial. "She thought their presence might be appropriate, given what Nina sacrificed for them."

Jordan nodded, recognizing the child psychologist who had worked with Nina in her final days. Beside her stood three young people—two girls and a boy, ranging from perhaps eleven to fifteen. Their expressions carried solemnity beyond their years, yet lacked the vacant quality Jordan had come to recognize in Hayes's vessels.

"They're doing well," Bella assured her, following her gaze. "The neural blocking frequency has been refined to target specific programming pathways without affecting normal development. And with Caine gone, the immediate threat of network reconstruction has been eliminated."

Victor Caine had died six weeks after his capture—not from any external cause, but from what medical examiners termed "catastrophic neural cascade failure." The severing of Hayes's network, combined with the continuous neural blocking frequency, had ultimately destroyed the pathways his brain had relied upon. His death had marked the final dissolution of the immediate threat, though vigilance remained essential.

"Madam President."

Jordan turned to find Jasper Reed approaching slowly, supported by a cane but otherwise appearing remarkably recovered. The neural damage from Hayes's possession had initially mirrored Nina's condition, yet the former president had gradually regained function—perhaps because his connection to the network had been more recent, less integrated into his developing neural architecture.

"Jasper." Jordan took his outstretched hand. "I'm glad you could be here."

"I wouldn't miss it," he replied, his voice carrying genuine emotion. "That young woman saved me from a darkness I never knew existed within my own mind. The least I can do is honor her sacrifice."

As they spoke, Jordan observed Theo making his way toward them, his usual easy charm subdued but present. The past three months had transformed their working relationship in ways neither could have anticipated. The dual operations that night had established a partnership beyond political calculation—the President and Vice President functioning truly as a unified executive.

"They're ready to begin," Theo informed them quietly. "The military honor guard is in position."

Jordan nodded, moving with Michael toward their designated seats at the front. As they settled, she felt rather than saw the subtle shift in the gathered crowd—thousands of citizens who had traveled to witness this moment, their attention coalescing as the ceremony prepared to commence.

The memorial service proceeded with dignified precision. The military honor guard presented colors with solemn reverence. Religious leaders offered prayers from diverse traditions. Musical selections—chosen by the children at Nina's orphanage—provided moments of reflection between speakers.

When Jordan's turn came to address the gathering, she approached the podium with measured steps. The speech she had prepared and memorized felt suddenly inadequate in the face of Nina's ultimate gift. She set her notes aside, choosing instead to speak directly from her heart.

"Nina Foster was fourteen years old," she began, her voice carrying across the hushed cemetery. "She should have been worried about school dances and homework assignments. Instead, she carried a burden none of us can truly comprehend—the weight of another consciousness imposed upon her own."

Jordan paused, gathering herself.

"Three months ago, Nina made a choice that saved our democracy. When confronted with the full power of Hayes's network, she chose to sever connections she had carried since infancy. She chose freedom—not just for herself, but for every vessel in Hayes's design. And she did so knowing the cost."

Throughout the audience, Jordan could see tissues being raised to eyes, heads bowing in acknowledgment of sacrifice.

"The easy path would be to call Nina a hero and leave it at that. To suggest her sacrifice was somehow part of a grand design. But the harder truth is that Nina should never have been placed in that position. She was a child used as a weapon in games she never chose."

Jordan's gaze found the three young people sitting beside Dr. Reeves—survivors of Hayes's programming, their lives forever altered but now reclaimed.

"Our responsibility—to Nina and to every child affected by Hayes's designs—is to ensure this never happens again. The Nina Foster Foundation represents our commitment to that promise. Every child identified and treated, every vessel freed from influence they never chose, honors what Nina gave us with her final act."

As Jordan concluded her remarks, she noticed something she hadn't seen before—a small wooden box placed beside the podium. Understanding dawned as she recognized the craftsmanship. The children from Nina's orphanage had created a container for mementos, to be sealed within the memorial's foundation.

After returning to her seat, Jordan watched as various speakers approached, each adding personal perspective to the collective remembrance. Senator Harper spoke eloquently about the nature of sacrifice and the courage required to confront uncomfortable truths. Theo Marshall emphasized the continued vigilance necessary to protect what Nina had preserved.

Throughout the ceremony, Jordan found herself reflecting on the journey that had led them here. From inauguration day's celebration to the desperate Senate confrontation, her presidency had been defined by the pursuit of truth that others couldn't—or wouldn't—acknowledge. The glass ceiling she had broken had indeed revealed darkness beyond imagination, just as Hayes had planned. Yet in that darkness, they had found not just threat but revelation—about the nature of consciousness, about the resilience of the human mind, about the capacity for redemption.

The Supreme Court's unanimous ruling on the Database Act had come just three weeks earlier. With Jordan's full support, the justices had declared the legislation unconstitutional in its original form, while preserving narrowly tailored provisions for identifying neural programming signatures. The system of checks and balances had functioned exactly as designed—correcting overreach while acknowledging legitimate security concerns.

As the ceremony neared its conclusion, Dr. Reeves approached the podium with one of her young charges—a girl of perhaps twelve, with solemn eyes and carefully braided hair.

"Emma Collins was one of the children recovered from Caine's facility," Dr. Reeves explained. "She has asked to share a few words."

The girl stepped forward, her small hands gripping a folded paper that trembled slightly. When she spoke, her voice carried surprising strength.

"I never met Nina Foster," she began. "But I know she's the reason I can think my own thoughts now. The reason the voice in my head is just mine." Emma glanced down at her paper, then set it aside, choosing to speak directly as Jordan had done. "The doctors explained that Nina broke the connections that made us all like puppets. That she knew doing it would hurt her really bad, but she did it anyway."

Emma's gaze swept across the gathered dignitaries, finding Jordan's face with unexpected directness.

"I wanted to say thank you. Not just to Nina, but to everyone who didn't give up looking for us. Who believed us when we said something was wrong inside our heads." Her voice caught slightly. "I'm going to school again next month. Regular school. With friends and homework and everything normal. Nina gave me that."

As Emma returned to her seat, Jordan felt something break loose within her chest—grief mingled with profound validation. Everything they had risked—her presidency, her reputation, the nation's stability—had been worth this moment. Worth seeing this child reclaiming the normal life Hayes had attempted to steal.

When the ceremonial portion concluded, attendees were invited to approach the memorial individually. Jordan waited, allowing others to go before her. She watched as the three children placed handwritten notes in the wooden box. As Senator Harper and Bella each left small tokens of remembrance. As Jasper Reed stood in silent contemplation before Nina's likeness.

Finally, when most guests had begun to disperse, Jordan approached the memorial alone. The silver key brooch felt warm in her palm as she withdrew it from her pocket. The small card that had accompanied it on inauguration day had read: "For the woman who unlocked the highest door. With respect and admiration."

Jordan traced the brooch's outline with her finger before placing it gently in the wooden box. The symbol felt appropriate beyond words—the key that had opened one door revealing another, far more consequential. The presidency that began with breaking a glass ceiling had transformed into something no one could have anticipated.

"She would have appreciated that," Michael said quietly, joining her at the memorial. "The symbolism."

Jordan nodded, unable to speak past the emotion tightening her throat. They stood together in silence, the spring breeze carrying cherry blossom petals across the cemetery's immaculate grounds.

"Ready?" Michael asked finally, offering his arm.

As they turned to leave, Jordan noticed Emma standing near the path, watching the presidential couple with undisguised curiosity. The girl's mother—a woman Jordan recognized as one of the Foundation's volunteer coordinators—stood nearby, allowing her daughter this moment of connection.

Jordan approached them, Secret Service adjusting smoothly to accommodate her detour.

"Hello, Emma," she said, extending her hand. "Thank you for your words today. They meant a great deal to everyone who heard them."

The girl shook her hand with surprising firmness. "Dr. Reeves says I might be able to help other kids someday. Because I understand what it's like to have someone else in your head."

"I believe you will," Jordan replied. "And the Nina Foster Foundation will be there to support that work."

Emma nodded, solemn beyond her years yet carrying something Nina had never been able to reclaim—possibility. Future unopened by premature sacrifice.

"Madam President?" Emma asked hesitantly. "Do you think it's really over? All the bad stuff that happened?"

Jordan considered the question carefully, weighing the complex truth against what this child needed to hear.

"Hayes's direct influence has ended," she answered honestly. "But understanding what he discovered—about consciousness, about neural programming—that work continues. The difference is that now we're pursuing it openly, ethically, with proper oversight."

"And with people who got to choose," Emma added with unexpected insight.

"Exactly," Jordan smiled, recognizing wisdom beyond the girl's years. "Choice makes all the difference."

As Jordan rejoined Michael and they walked toward the waiting motorcade, she felt a subtle shift within herself—not the disappearance of grief or responsibility, but their transformation into something constructive. The presidency that had nearly collapsed under accusations of paranoia now stood validated before history. The investigation that had consumed resources and credibility had ultimately saved democracy itself.

The cherry blossoms continued their gentle descent, coating the pathways with petals that resembled fresh snow despite the spring warmth.

Jordan paused to watch this natural cycle—beauty emerging, then falling, making way for whatever came next. Nina's memorial would stand permanently in this place of honor, but the truest memorial to her sacrifice lived in the recovered children, in the Foundation's ongoing work, in a government that had faced impossible truth and emerged stronger.

"What are you thinking?" Michael asked, noticing her contemplative expression.

Jordan watched as Emma and her mother placed one final flower at the base of Nina's memorial before walking hand-in-hand toward their future.

"That some ceilings need to be broken," she answered quietly. "Even when we don't know what lies beyond."

The spring sun broke through passing clouds, illuminating the cemetery in sudden, brilliant clarity. Jordan Prescott, the President who had pursued truth at nearly unbearable cost, turned her face toward the light and allowed herself to believe in what might yet emerge from darkness revealed.

Also by Denis James

The Arcane Rebellion Series:

Tobias – Book One

Hunter – Book Two

Aurora – Book Three (Coming Soon!)

Chapter One
Showdown at Jefferson High

It was a dark and stormy afternoon in a high school classroom overlooking a large parking lot and an array of trees. It was nearly the end of a long September day on a Friday afternoon at Jefferson High School. Football season was here, but there was a feeling of disappointment at the cancellation of the homecoming football game that had been scheduled for that evening. As it turns out, even high school sports are at the mercy of Mother Nature.

Sixteen students sat at their desks, occasionally looking up from their test papers just long enough to check the clock at the front of the room. Or spare a glance at their teacher, Mr. Tobias Thornfield, who was grading papers in the front of the room. There were less than five minutes left to go until the bell rang, signaling the end of the day and freedom for two glorious days. The test was difficult, the room was stuffy, and there was a general feeling of apprehension throughout the room.

Mr. Thornfield looked up from his papers to check on the students. He observed pencils scribbling as though their owners' lives depended on the outcome. He frowned as he looked at the faces of the students in front of him.

The students were unsure and nervous, and it couldn't be plainer that they didn't feel prepared for this test. Of course, this wasn't particularly a surprise for Mr. Thornfield. He had long since abandoned the idea that school would come as easily to his students as it had seemed to for him.

Mr. Thornfield was not an old teacher by any stretch of the imagination, but neither was he particularly young. While there were many peculiar things about this man, his appearance was anything but. A short, thin man with long, black hair, he did not seem to take very good care of himself. His hair was rather greasy and unkempt, and it was obvious he hadn't bathed for a few days. His clothes were a little dirty and disheveled, as though he had simply picked them up off the floor that morning and put them on. After a first glance, most people walking by would not give Mr. Thornfield a second one.

Despite his lackluster appearance, the students in this teacher's class seemed to respect him well enough. While his was a challenging subject (an upperclassman course in English literature) Mr. Thornfield was an excellent teacher. The students, and staff, at Jefferson High School all knew of his excellence. He would pass through the hallways, and students would show excitement at the upcoming lesson for the day, and staff would praise him for happenings in his classroom. When hearing uplifting comments like this, Mr. Thornfield shrugged them off; it didn't matter to him what students thought of him or his teaching style, and he cared even less what his colleagues thought. Only one thing mattered to him.

Mr. Thornfield was not an ordinary man. He had a secret, one that nobody at this school could learn until the very end of his tenure there. The organization he worked for had entrusted him to find new recruits for their mission. High school students were, of course, the most easily persuadable for this venture. They sought action, adventure, and excitement. But they were mature enough to recognize their own limits, unlike those irritating younger kids. By the time they hit college age, they were almost too mature; trying to convince a college student to join his organization was by no means impossible, but in his experience, they had a much firmer grasp on what exactly they wanted out of their lives than high school students did and thus were less likely to commit. For it was a lifelong commitment to Bellwater. You did not simply resign or retire; you were enlisted, and you stayed with the organization.

Mr. Thornfield checked his watch. The bell was due to ring in less than thirty seconds.

"Pencils down, everyone!"

There was a general murmur of anxiety rustling through the classroom at these words—the first words spoken in the classroom since Mr. Thornfield had passed out the exams forty minutes prior. Mr. Thornfield rolled his eyes inwardly.

"Calm down, everyone! We'll pick this back up on Monday. Give me your tests on your way out the door! If a test leaves this room, it's a zero."

At these words, the entire class breathed a sigh of relief. There were even some "yippies" thrown in there from a few brave souls. At this, Mr. Thornfield really did roll his eyes.

"Yes, yes, but do make sure you review more carefully

over the weekend, yes?"

"Yes, Mr. Thornfield," several members of the class chirped back in happiness.

The bell rang thirty seconds later. The students packed up their bags hurriedly, threw their tests at Mr. Thornfield, and left to enjoy a weekend that would undoubtedly be filled with memories that Mr. Thornfield didn't want, or need, to ever find out about.

"Mr. Thornfield?"

Mr. Thornfield looked up; two of the students had stayed behind: Foxton Gray and Finnian Connor. Foxton was a tall student, a senior boy with flaming red hair and freckles covering his pale face. Finnian was a short boy, also a senior, with curly black hair and tan skin. The two boys could not look any more different, yet they were best friends. Or at least, Mr. Thornfield had assumed they were, as they were almost always together.

"Yes?" asked the teacher.

"We just wanted to tell you we think you're doing a great job!" exclaimed Foxton, beaming. He handed his test to his teacher, grinned at Finnian, and walked out of the room with his friend behind him.

Mr. Thornfield shook his head, not really getting the joke. But he didn't think much of it. He tossed the tests into a pile on his crowded desk—he really was an overworked teacher—and started getting ready to leave.

After all, it was the weekend for him, too, and he had plenty of stuff to do.

Foxton and Finnian were two of Mr. Thornfield's favorites. Every teacher, no matter who they are or what they tell you, is going to have favorite students. Foxton Gray was mischievous and had gotten on Mr. Thornfield's nerves on more than one occasion despite the fact that it was literally the third week of school. He was outgoing and popular, and earned good grades for himself, but the thing Mr. Thornfield liked most about Foxton was that he was genuinely very kind. He had met more than one popular student who thought they were way too popular for hanging out with students who were unpopular. But Foxton wasn't that kid; he would take the unpopular kid under his wing and build them up instead of tearing them down.

Finnian was one of those "unpopular" kids that Foxton took under his wing. Relatively quiet and not at all outgoing, Finnian was also the smartest kid in the room. Foxton—even though he got good grades—was not someone whom Mr. Thornfield would have considered book-smart. He earned good grades mainly from extreme effort and more talented friends, at least when it came to academics. Hence, Finnian Connor. A frontrunner to be valedictorian with his graduating class, Finnian had earned full-ride scholarships to several Ivy League schools.

Mr. Thornfield's thoughts were interrupted when a blood-curdling, glass-shattering scream pierced his eardrums. He looked up towards the door of the classroom, frowning. It was not unusual for him to hear strange, random noises coming from the hallway–high school students were unpredictable in that regard–but something about this seemed odd to him. He strode over to the doorway and didn't even make it before the one scream soon turned into two, and then several. Then, he felt something he never expected to feel in his classroom.

He felt intense heat and smoke coming from the first floor of the school. Students and staff alike were running, trying to get away from the source of it all, but it was no use; the heat and smoke were soon followed by red-orange flames. The fire was spreading quickly; it danced from one end of the building to the next, engulfing everything in its path. Desks, lockers, chairs, even people were swallowed by the fire as though they were nothing.

Mr. Thornfield hesitated, standing at the door to his classroom. The fire was spreading quickly...too quickly. A natural fire did not spread this fast.

A man materialized, seemingly out of thin air, at the end of the hallway where Mr. Thornfield's classroom was located, directly in front of Foxton and Finnian. The two boys, startled, jumped in midair at the sight of the man. This man was masked, covered head to toe in a black robe. Beyond the fact that he was of average size, it was impossible to make out his face or any distinguishing features. The man had not yet noticed Foxton and Finnian; he was facing away from them, looking at a small group of teenage girls who were trying to find a way around the flames.

The man laughed, a cold, merciless laugh that ran shivers down Mr. Thornfield's spine. Then the man snapped his fingers, and fire–pure, unfiltered fire–rained down upon the girls, engulfing them instantly. One of the girls screamed, but it was a short scream before it was instantly silenced. The girl had died a brutal, painful death.

Mr. Thornfield now knew what was going on…and he knew what he had to do. He had his orders: he was to protect the students he was preparing for the academy at all costs. The Bellwater Mages demanded that of him.

The man turned and noticed Foxton and Finnian, who were both frozen in terror, looking at the man. Foxton–the idiot boy–had pulled out his phone and started calling for emergency services, but Mr. Thornfield knew it was no use. Those boys were going to perish. Unless he did something to intervene.

So he did.

Tobias Thornfield snapped his fingers at the same instant that the man did. Fire, just like before with the girls, started to rain down upon Foxton and Finnian. But this time, the boys were not engulfed in flames. Instead, the boys were engulfed by a cloud of electricity that seemingly appeared from their pockets, protecting them from the flames. However, the madman who had cast the flames didn't realize their screams signaled they were alive, unlike those girls he had burned just moments before.

Tobias noticed the man was standing directly below a fully functioning light that had not yet been affected by the fire. He snapped his fingers again, and a bolt of lightning struck down upon the man who was casting the fire. He was sent flying and was knocked off the landing from the strength of the electricity, and slammed head-first to the floor below. Students screamed and ran away from the limp body on the floor below as he fell, landing hard. His body lay motionless on the floor.

The fire that was raining down upon Foxton and Finnian subsided. The boys went silent and looked around in disbelief; the school was still burning, and many people were still trapped. Tobias ran over to them.

"Don't ask questions!" he snapped at them as though that was their first inclination. He grabbed them both and pulled them closer to him. "Just wait for me…I'll be there soon."

Both boys vanished into thin air as suddenly as the man from before had appeared from nothing. Tobias looked around; his suspicion was that there was someone else who was causing the fire still to be found. His suspicion was proven correct when a man's voice suddenly carried from down below.

"Avery…Avery, what happened to you?!"

Tobias looked down below. The man whom he had knocked unconscious with a bolt of lightning was joined by two more men. One of the men looked vaguely familiar to Tobias, though it was impossible to tell any distinguishing features about this man from a distance.

"They must've overpowered him!" the unfamiliar man, who was slightly overweight and balding, screamed. He pointed towards a group of teachers running by. The teachers were instantly lit ablaze; they didn't even scream as they were engulfed in an instant. Another teacher nearby to them pulled the fire extinguisher off the wall, turned it on his colleagues, and sprayed it. The teachers were coated in a fire suppressant, but it did nothing.

Tobias vanished, and reappeared right behind the teachers who were ablaze. He had not been particularly close to any of his colleagues; after all, it was his first-year teaching at this school, and his teaching placements never tended to last very long. But he couldn't let them burn alive…he had to try and save them.

Tobias noticed a sprinkler up above where the teachers lay; the fire had not started the sprinkler system. He waved his hand towards the sprinkler, and water came gushing out of it as though he had just moved a giant boulder that was blocking its path. The water– which ordinarily would do nothing against this particular fire–was enhanced with magic, so it quickly put the fire out. But it was too late. The only thing left of the teachers were blackened, charred bodies that lay in the middle of the floor. Tobias sighed, and looked around for the two men, along with the unconscious man called Avery.

The smoke and heat were getting to be too much for Tobias. Everywhere he looked, students, teachers, even parents who had come running into the school trying to save their children lay on the floor, either dead or very nearly so. The fire alarm was going off, and he distantly heard the sound of fire trucks and ambulances, but he knew they would be too late. But if he could save just three more people…he would have all five new recruits for his organization.

And somehow, miraculously, he found them. But he wasn't the first to find them.

The two men from before were standing in front of a group of students. The overweight man was holding the unconscious man Tobias had struck down earlier on his back. The students standing before them were two girls and one boy. The two girls were Lyra and Elena Wilkins; both of them were juniors in Mr. Thornfield's class and had just been taking their exams. They were identical twins, both with long brown hair and were the stars of the girls' basketball team. The boy was named Darian Keen; Tobias didn't know much about him, but he was a short, skinny, blond boy. He was not part of any sports or any club; as far as Mr. Thornfield knew, Darian was a total outcast.

The two men then spoke to the students. What they said made shivers run down Tobias's spine despite the fact that he was standing in a blazing building surrounded by smoke. It wasn't just what they said, however.

"You three! Come here, and we will take you to safety! You will be joining us."

He recognized that voice; it was Hunter Diaz. Hunter was someone who he had been searching for for a long time. He never expected, nor wanted, to run into him here of all places, especially not while there was a building full of innocent people being burned alive due to Hunter and his friends' actions. Tobias clenched his fists.

"What are you talking about? Why would we go with

you? We don't even know you!"

"Girlie, you don't have much of a choice. Either come with us or be burned alive just like your friends!"

Lyra, Elena, and Darian didn't move. They were staring at Hunter, petrified.

"Is that how you want it? Fine!"

Hunter, a young, strong man of Mexican descent, with short black hair and black eyes, gathered an arm full of fire. The flames danced around him, obeying his every command. It didn't seem to harm him; on the contrary, it seemed to give him more life and purpose. He laughed, and Tobias knew what he needed to do. The flames lunged forward, directly toward Lyra, Elena, and Darian. Once again, Tobias disappeared and reappeared directly in front of the students.

At the exact same time of his reappearance, a tornado appeared in the middle of the hallway, in the space separating the men from the students. The tornado appeared seemingly out of nowhere and had been summoned by Tobias snapping his fingers at the exact moment he had reappeared. The tornado was quickly engulfed by flames, and then the flames were extinguished; the speed at which the tornado was blowing around was such that the fire was put out. Hunter and the other man stared incredulously at the tornado, then turned and spotted Tobias. Hunter gasped.

"Tobias!"

"What are you doing here, Hunter?" asked Tobias. He was livid; the last time he had seen Hunter, it had been under similar circumstances. But never did he imagine that Hunter would do something this destructive.

The tornado died out, and they were now surrounded by heat, flames, smoke, and ash.

"I could ask the same of you, Tobias."

"I happen to work here. Or at least I did, till you burned the place to the ground."

"The place was a dump anyway. You're better off if you ask me."

"I didn't."

Hunter glared at him.

"So, what are you doing here, Hunter? Just burning down schools for the hell of it now?"

"I suppose I'm here for the same reason you are. Recruitment, right?"

Tobias didn't have time to react to this statement; twenty feet away, part of the roof fell in. Evidently, the building was starting to collapse from the flames. The English teacher could hear water being pumped towards the school; the firefighters had arrived on the scene. But it wouldn't do anyone any good.

Tobias made a split-second decision: he needed to protect these kids, no matter the cost. Aurora was counting on him. He and Hunter had history, but that was all it was at this point: history. He punched the air, and instantly, a powerful gust of wind smashed head-first into Hunter and the other two men.

The three men were blasted backward off their feet. Hunter smashed head-first into a trophy case and was soon pummeled by various awards that students from the school had won over the years. The other two men flew towards a nearby window, smashing it to pieces and continuing to soar into the grounds of the burning school, out of sight.

Tobias turned around to face the students behind him.

"Lyra! Elena! Darian!" he shouted towards them.

They looked at him, shock and fear evident on their faces.

"Come here!" he gestured, indicating they should get closer. "Quickly now!"

Just like with Foxton and Finnian, he pulled the two girls into a giant bear hug. Then they disappeared.

It was just Darian and Tobias now. But just then, the ceiling of the school collapsed right on top of them.

Dust, rubble, smoke, heat, and flames engulfed both Tobias and Darian. Tobias, with a quick flick of his wrist, was surrounded by six mini-tornadoes. The tornadoes blew the remains of the school ceiling away from him, and kept the flames, smoke, and ash at bay as well, though it did little for the heat. Darian, however, had smashed into the floor and after one quick scream, became lifeless and made no more movements nor sound.

Tobias swore; then he stretched out his arm, pointed at the spot where Darian had been moments ago, and waved his hand. Instantly, a powerful gust of wind blew the remains of the roof off Darian's lifeless body. The roof went flying right into Tobias's classroom. Tobias grabbed Darian, and vanished, leaving behind nothing but a destroyed high school and hundreds of dead bodies.

Connect with Denis James

Denis James has a true passion for all things mental health related. A (recovering) chronic depression and severe anxiety patient, Denis James writes with the intention of helping others who may be where he once was. When not writing, Denis can be seen teaching in his community (usually something IT-related, though he has also taught business/marketing, finance, hospitality, and more), nerding out (his favorite fandoms include Pokemon, Harry Potter, Yu-Gi-Oh, and Kingdom Hearts), planning travel, or being home with his family.

Connect with Denis James:

- Facebook: Denis James – Writer

- Instagram: denisjameswriter

- Twitter: denisjameswrite

- Patreon: Denis James – Writer

www.ingramcontent.com/pod-product-compliance
Lightning Source LLC
Chambersburg PA
CBHW030141010826
48973CB00002B/676